Il Padrino:
The Godfather

Il Padrino: The Godfather

JACK LANGLEY

IL PADRINO: THE GODFATHER

This is a work of fiction. All of the characters, names, incidents, organizations, and dialogue in this novel are either the products of the author's imagination or are used fictitiously.

iUniverse books may be ordered through booksellers or by contacting:

iUniverse
1663 Liberty Drive
Bloomington, IN 47403
www.iuniverse.com
1-800-Authors (1-800-288-4677)

Because of the dynamic nature of the Internet, any web addresses or links contained in this book may have changed since publication and may no longer be valid. The views expressed in this work are solely those of the author and do not necessarily reflect the views of the publisher, and the publisher hereby disclaims any responsibility for them.

Any people depicted in stock imagery provided by Thinkstock are models, and such images are being used for illustrative purposes only.
Certain stock imagery © Thinkstock.

ISBN: 978-1-4917-8251-4 (sc)
ISBN: 978-1-4917-8252-1 (e)

Library of Congress Control Number: 2015918566

Print information available on the last page.

iUniverse rev. date: 11/17/2015

PROLOGUE

A lifetime of anticipation was nearing its end. At long last, he was about to arrive in the land of his ancestors. Delta's flight 64 from Atlanta to Rome had departed Hartsfield-Jackson airport on time. Having encountered turbulence shortly after the flight left the North American airspace east of Labrador, it was now destined to be about thirty minutes late arriving at its destination. The almost two hour period of sporadic turmoil had created apprehension among passengers and crew alike. Finally, as dawn was peeking from behind the pillars of darkness, the northern coast of Ireland came into view and the roughness ceased. While the airship slipped smoothly and quietly across England, France and Switzerland, the passengers were finally able to enjoy breakfast served just after seven a.m. local time.

As the A-330 jumbo jet passed over the majestic snow capped peaks of the Alps, it entered Italian airspace. And as it began its gentle descent into Rome's Fiumicino Airport, the flight attendants passed through the crowded coach cabin offering warm facial towels. Following the all night flight, the scented moisture and the gentle heat were at least as welcome as the hearty dark-brewed Starbucks coffee served during breakfast and beyond with unlimited refills offered the java enthusiasts.

It would be his first time in Italy. He had heard stories about the old country from his family since he was a child. He had been told that his grandparents had emigrated from Campania to America in the 1890's and had lived in New York prior to moving to central Connecticut in the early part of the twentieth century. The question of why they had left Italy had never been addressed.

¯And to this very day, he could not comprehend why not one of that generation had ever returned to the Italian homeland once they were safely ensconced on America's shore. Surely, there must have been relatives, friends and memories that should have beckoned them to return.

Yet none of the succeeding generations...until now...had ever set foot on any Italian soil let alone the ancestral homes of Eboli and Campagna in the Campania region's Salerno Province. Perhaps this voyage of discovery would finally answer the question...***why not***?

With the Tyrrhenian Sea visible through the portals to the west, the jumbo jet made its final approach and set down smoothly on the runway. Eager to begin the journey south, his pulse was racing as he stepped from the plane onto the jetway and then into the terminal. Two to three hours from Rome's Fiumicino airport to the outskirts of Naples is what his tour books suggested as the average driving time. Armed with a MapQuest app on the iPhone in his pocket, he was ready to tackle the unfamiliar route outlined on its maps.

His suitcase was circling on the carousel as he approached the designated baggage claim area. With his luggage in tow, he proceeded to customs where clearance was thankfully a mere formality. Then began the lengthy walk to the car rental kiosks through a series of tunnel-like corridors and overhead walkways that led from the terminal to the car rental facility directly across the street.

The interminable hassle required to rent a car on foreign soil that followed reminded him of just how accessible things were back home in the good old U.S.A. Yes, he would be going near Naples. No, he could not drive a Fiat there as originally planned since it is the number one brand of car stolen in the country. Did he want additional insurance leaving him a zero balance due in the event of damage or theft? You bet since his insurance and credit card wouldn't cover those items in Italy. So he had settled for the brand new Kia offered instead. He silently laughed as he considered the irony of the whole situation: flying thousands of miles from America to Italy to drive a car made in South Korea.

Forty-five minutes later, he was finally set. He was tired, but the excitement of the long awaited adventure would keep him alert while he negotiated the A1 highway toward Naples, circled the incomparable Mount Vesuvius, and traveled east on the A3 which would lead him through the Campania region and eventually into Salerno Province containing the home towns of his forebears.

As he drove, he glanced at the paper he held tightly clenched in his right hand. It had been given to him by his Uncle Tony, a copy of a letter written in early 1925 by a great uncle, Thomas Catalano, from Philadelphia…printed on stationery from the Sons of Italy Bank. It recounted the family ancestry that had originated in Spain some five centuries earlier with **Don Gaetano Catalano, the Marquis of Gonzales,** the progenitor of the family, who had immigrated to Italy as Chief of Staff to Don Pedro of Toledo, emissary of King Charles V of Spain. It was Don Gaetano Catalano and his descendents whom he now sought on this quest for answers to a cluster of plaguing questions. Little could he anticipate the life changing surprises that lay in store or the perils that his visit would ignite.

THE SONS OF ITALY STATE BANK & TRUST COMPANY

N.W. COR. BROAD AND TASKER STREETS

PHILADELPHIA

ROBERT LOMBARDI, PRESIDENT
JOHN H. DI SILVESTRO, FIRST VICE PRES.
DR FORTUNATO VITANZA, SECOND VICE PRES.
LOUIS CORONA, CASHIER
GINO PAPOLA, ASSISTANT CASHIER

May 3rd 1925.

Dear Nephew:

In answer to your letter of the 27th last, I will try my best in giving the information you desire, in what my memory only can help me, because I have here no documentary cards at all.

By research made by me long years ago, when I was in Italy, I find that the ancestor of our family came in Italy from Spain in the 15th century, as chief of staff of Don Pedro of Toledo, Vice King of Spain for the Kingdom of Naples. His name was Don Gaetano Catalano, Marquis of Gonzales. He procreated many children, but I suppose you know that in the past time only the first son have the right to the title and the property of the family, and the other sons, which were called cadets, do not deserve nothing. Our family had its origin by one of these cadets, born in the city of Monteleone in Calabria, and then transferred at Campagna as capo guardacaccia in the royal wood of Persano. By this ancestor derived our family in Campagna, and the other families established at Controne and at Serre di Persano, two small town in the same provine of Salerno.

The hereditary descendent of the first branch, with the title of Marquis of Gonzales, was living in Naples in a magnificent palace of the Riviera di Chiaia. I know him long years ago and talk with him. His name was the same as that of our first ancestor, namely Don Gaetano Catalano Marquis of Gonzales, and by him I collect many news about our family and get the coat-of-arms seen by you in one of my name cards.

This is all I can recollect about our ancestors, and hope what I say before will please you. I am well and hope the same for all member of your family. My best regard to your father and mother, sisters and brother.

Your uncle

Thomas Catalano

Thomas Catalano

Editor
T. J. T. R. Catalano   Philadelphia

PART ONE

CHAPTER ONE

From Rome, he drove south towards Naples, capital city of the region of Campania, containing the ancestral homes of his grandmother and grandfather, Eboli and Campagna respectively.

Campania is a region in the central southwest coast of the Italian peninsula, comprising almost 14,000 sq km. Although it is only 12th in ranking by regional size, constituting only 4.5% of Italy's land mass, by population it is second only to the Rome metropolitan complex. With almost six million inhabitants, it has the highest population density of any area in the country.

The name Campania originates from the Latin phrase *campania felix* or "fortunate countryside". Its name is equivalent to Champagne, the famous grape producing region of France.

Originally part of the Magna Graecia, or Great Greek colonies, the earliest settlement was at Cumae, north of the present day regional capital, Naples. Occupied in the 8th century B.C., its earliest settlers, the Etruscans and Samnites, gave way to the Roman occupation by the 3rd century, B.C. Hannibal attempted to provoke the Romans into abandoning the region. After his success at the battle of Cannae in 216 B.C., Capua (later home to the famous gladiatorial schools and an early major city of the region) seceded and attempted to acquire equality of governance from Rome. Despite Hannibal's pledge of help, he was absent in 211 B.C. when the Romans succeeded in starving the city into submission.

Campania would remain Rome's principal breadbasket for centuries until Egypt became its major supplier of grains. Following that event, the Campania region would sequentially be acquired by the Goths, the Byzantine Empire, the Spanish, the Lombards and eventually by the French Bourbon dynasty in 1713 as part of the "Kingdom of the Two Sicilies."

Around 1815, movement toward a united Italy began. In the 1840's, Giuseppe Mazzini spearheaded a movement for Italian independence. Sicily was the first state to declare a constitution. The Austrians continued to disrupt plans for further unity when they conquered the Piedmontese. Count Camillo de Cavour became Prime Minister of Sardinia in 1852 and rapidly aided in the unification movement. Aided by Giuseppe Garibaldi and a French alliance, the Austrians were finally forced out.

Finally, on March 12, 1861, in Turin (capital of Piedmont-Sardinia), Italian reunification…"*Risorgimento*"… was essentially complete. On that date, the Kingdom of Italy was proclaimed by a parliament representing all the Italian states except Venetiae, which remained under Austrian control until 1866, and Rome, which remained under Papal control until 1870. Victor Emmanuel was proclaimed the first king of the unified Italy and Rome became capital of the newly united country in July of 1871.

CHAPTER TWO

As he made his way toward Eboli, the view to the west reminded him of Hawaii: the proximity of the mountain slopes to the sandy shoreline, the deep blue waters of the Tyrrhenian Sea shimmering in the distance, and palm trees swaying to gentle breezes.

Directly ahead of him to the east, however, he was surprised by the height of the mountain ranges. He had read the name Apennines numerous times in history books and had seen it displayed on the maps of Italy he had studied before undertaking his present journey. He had even researched the name's origin... penne in Latin...that translated as quill or feather that gave root to the word pinnacle...a word that befitted the towering majesty that now stretched out before him.

His thoughts about the strength and endurance of the many armies that had marched throughout the region were magnified at the sight. Somehow, all the stories about the Roman legions under Caesar, and the Carthaginians led by Hannibal...and the rebellious slave army led by Spartacus...were now undergoing updating in his memory by what he was observing in real time.

He had often tried to envision the difficulties endured by these defenders and opponents of the realm during their respective eras. But now, that effort had taken on Herculean proportions. Marching tens or hundreds of miles on relatively flat terrain and then fighting a battle would have been daunting enough. But negotiating the mountainous terrain he was seeing for the first time...and then fighting in hand-to-hand combat gave him pause.

"I'm glad that I'm finally getting the chance to see the birthplace of my ancestors firsthand," he thought.

"This place is truly awe inspiring."

*

Thoughts of California and Florida came to mind as he passed numerous citrus groves of oranges and lemons en route to his grandmother's hometown. He was surprised to see numerous commercial canning plants in the immediate area of Eboli during his approach, bearing names that he recognized from the tomato products that both he and his mother had used for making sauces for various pasta dishes.

The town was fairly quiet and old...but neither as ancient nor as quaint as he had visualized it in his mind's eye all these years. Having quickly passed through the business area of town on a crescent shaped drive that was now heading southeast back towards the A-3, he suddenly stopped and made a quick U-turn. The sign post he had just passed said Campagna on it... he was reasonably sure.

All the maps and internet sites had located it in proximity to Eboli, but there had been little in the way of any definitive directions or information.

And suddenly there it was. He had been correct in his sighting.

Campagna...eight kilometers.

Five miles!

His heart raced as he drove past the picket fence sign and turned toward the direction it indicated. Finally, he would see his grandfather Felix Catalano's home town.

The road quickly turned into a steep pass with an unprotected edge jutting out over a precipice at least a thousand feet above a canyon floor as it proceeded into a crevice between two mountain ranges that converged at an almost sixty degree angle. It was little wonder that time had essentially forgotten the town. It was but a small village with a single road that circled past homes, a few shops and the obligatory Catholic Church on its way back to rejoin the same road that had brought him from Eboli. A small river, identified as the Tenza by a small signpost, flowed through the town's center and to the east narrow streets coursed up steep hills.

Due to a faulty signpost obviously turned in the wrong direction he discovered too late, he had dared to negotiate one of the hills only to find himself in a unique predicament: that portion of the village had streets so narrow that they would not accommodate even the relatively small rental car that he drove.

He couldn't help but recall scenes from the small mountainous village in the movie, ***The Godfather***, where Michael Corleone met and wed his ill-fated first wife, Appolonia. Only the armed protectori were missing. He mused that it must still look the same as it had a century and a half ago when his grandfather had lived here!

He carefully backed up and turned the vehicle around and made his way down the steep incline, to the main road. As he entered the main square, the Piazza Guerriero, he was somewhat surprised when an old woman beckoned to him as he passed the church.

Stopping, he tried to understand what she was saying in Italian, only to realize by her gestures that she was begging for a handout of cigarettes. He watched closely as she made a V with her fingers and slowly lifted it to her mouth. He couldn't help but notice that she only had a single crooked tooth that projected from her upper gum line.

Scenes from old World War II movies came to mind.

"GI's handed out candy to the children and cigarettes to the adults of the country being invaded", he thought.

He managed to convey to her that he was sorry but he didn't have any cigarettes…that he didn't smoke. "Io non fumo" he said to her after consulting his Italian dictionary. The forlorn look and almost toothless grimace signaled her disappointment. He waved and bade her "arrivederci" although he felt a measure of dissatisfaction by not being able to help her in some way, but continued his journey even though.

Circling back to his starting point, he sought a sign that he had noticed earlier when he first entered the town, indicating some sort of historical museum. Hoping he could find some information there about the Catalano family, he parked the car and entered the building.

Despite the letter he held from his late great uncle in Philadelphia, he knew relatively little else about his ancestry as no one in the immediate generations had shown any interest in such matters, and essentially knew no more than he...or cared not to volunteer it if they did. And he had not had time to research things to his satisfaction prior to embarking on this trip.

So armed with little more than a keen sense of adventure concerning the truth about his ancestors...be it good or bad...he began his quest when the greeter asked him how she could help... in Italian of course. He was somewhat prepared, carrying a pocket companion of **Spoken Italian Made Easy** with him.

"Io non parlo italiano molto bene." He slowly delivered the words in her native language after consulting the book.

She smiled and then welcomed him in fluent English.

"Your pronunciation is very good...molto bene" she said with a smile.

He was pleased to find that his host spoke his native language, making things remarkably easier for him. A striking woman, she introduced herself as Maria Rosato and confided that she was a native of the small town. She appeared to be of similar age...about thirty-five years old...and unlike most people of the region that he had so far observed, had good dentition, spoke with a quality that suggested advanced education, and dressed in clothes that indicated a moderate level of affluence. She stood about five feet five inches tall and bore a striking resemblance to one of Italy's favorite actresses, Sophia Loren.

Maria volunteered that she had been educated in Rome, and had returned to Naples where she had married, but unfortunately had been widowed several years earlier. She had remained there working in an antique bookstore until a sudden illness in her family had forced her to move home less than a year earlier. Her mother, who had been diagnosed with cancer, had rapidly succumbed to the disease less than a month prior to his visit.

She was working in the visitor's historical museum until she could get all her family's affairs taken care of at which time she indicated she would probably return either to Naples or Rome.

He was surprised by her candor and expressed his condolences over the recent loss of her mother. However, not wanting to dwell on her personal problems, he turned to matters that had brought him to Campagna.

He explained to her his dilemma about the Catalano family and showed her the letter from Thomas Catalano written in nineteen twenty-five.

"According to our records, there are still two people here in Campagna with your family name. I'm sorry that I don't know either of them. It is a small town as you can see, but I have been away for many years and according to my information both of these persons would be in their nineties. They must not have had children or I'm sure I would have recognized them. It's hard not to be aware of a name in a town of only about two thousand.

My records indicate numerous additional families named Catalano in the Campania region...but that covers a very large area including Naples."

"I'd appreciate a list of the names and any contact information that you can provide. I'd like to meet...or at least call...any or all of them and see if I can establish whether or not I'm related. Maybe they will know something about my ancestors beyond my grandparent's generation."

Maria smiled. "I'll be more than happy to make a list for you and place the calls. And, if you like, I can go with you to see any of them that might be relatives. I'd be delighted to be your translator. It's often difficult to get anywhere with local people who know no English and have never been outside the confines of Salerno or Italy."

"That would be wonderful. I'll be more than happy to pay you for your services." He was surprised and delighted at her response, not expecting such generosity from a stranger.

"That won't be necessary. The pleasure would be mine. It's time I got back to living my life and this would be a good start... meeting other people and participating in a little...shall we call it 'international diplomacy'?"

She couldn't help but be impressed by this American who stood at least six feet two inches tall, had wavy dark hair and eyes of brown. His skin was olive, suggesting that he had indeed inherited the Italian genes of the ancestors he sought. His suave mannerisms indicated to her that he was well bred and conceivably wealthy.

"You're on.

Sophia...I'm sorry...Maria, perhaps I can buy you dinner tonight if you're not too busy?"

She paused for a brief moment as if in thought, but then quickly responded.

"I'd like that.

And don't be embarrassed by calling me 'Sophia'. A lot of people make the same mistake. It's hard not to be flattered when being compared to someone so beautiful and so talented...especially when you're plain like me."

"I would have to take exception to that last statement" he quickly retorted as he eyed her features and silhouette once more.

"You're certainly anything but plain."

She smiled demurely but avoided any further comment or immediate eye contact.

And with that brief introduction, a new relationship had been born and the start of a lifetime adventure that neither could have foreseen only moments earlier had begun.

CHAPTER THREE

C harles V, King of Spain and recently proclaimed Holy Roman Emperor, relied heavily on his numerous viceroys to keep or restore order in his vast holdings that by 1530 included (in addition to Spain) portions of France, the Netherlands, Holland, Luxembourg, Austria and Italy.

Italy had been in disarray for centuries, especially in and around Naples where petty disputes, power brokering and infighting were an everyday problem among local barons. In addition, the plague of 1529 had left the city decimated and worse with an estimated 60,000 deaths attributed to the disease.

Charles had summoned one of his most trustworthy viceroys, Don Pedro of Toledo, and commanded him to take charge of Naples. Arriving there in September of 1532, Don Pedro became the Viceroy of Naples and quickly set to work to make Naples a formidable city among the Italian city-states and a valuable asset to the Kingdom of Spain.

Don Pedro Alvarez de Toledo

He immediately had his forces begin construction of his new residence, a palace christened Santa Chiara just west of the ancient Roman wall and along the newly constructed Riviera di Chiara (still a street along the modern day Bay of Naples).

"At your service, my Lord."

Don Gaetano Catalano, the Marquis of Gonzalez, removed his plumed hat, swinging it through an arc as he bowed to Don Pedro of Toledo.

"Don Gaetano, my compliments to you and your men on the progress you have made with my new residence and the barracks to house our men. Are you in a position to project when it may be complete?"

"My Lord, if the weather holds we hope to finish within this calendar year. As you know, since our arrival here we have been met with some unfortunate storms along the Bay that have kept us from being further along with the project."

"Yes, indeed.

The weather certainly has been less than cooperative.

Since you and your men have served me well, I have another assignment for you. As soon as those projects are complete, we will have need to construct additional buildings to hold court since the population here is rather rowdy and seems to enjoy tempting our authority."

"As you wish, my Lord. I will arrange a meeting for you with our architects so that they may begin formulating plans for such buildings right away. We can then begin construction as soon as these current projects are complete."

"You please me with your willingness to do my bidding, Don Gaetano."

"My Lord," Don Gaetano added as he bowed and backed out of the room.

*

The next two decades saw marked growth in Naples as Don Pedro's building plans came to fruition. In addition to the area around Santa Chiara that included a dozen blocks of new barracks, a square was erected that boasted the first multi-storied buildings in Europe. He authorized the modernization of fortresses along the coast, both north and south of Naples and built a new wall along the sea front. Naples became the best fortified city of its time under his leadership.

His harsh dealings with feudal barons in Naples and the surrounding countryside led to the breakup of large estate holdings and drove people into the city causing the population to swell to over two hundred thousand, making it the largest city in Italy and second only to Paris in all of Europe. With the marked increase in its numbers of citizens, he centralized administration and moved all the courts onto the same premises, the Castel Capuano...or Vicaria, now completed as promised by Don Gaetano.

In 1547, Charles V instructed Don Pedro to institute the Inquisition. He immediately summoned his trusty Chief of Staff.

"Don Gaetano, I have another undertaking for you as well. You can leave your regular duties to your capable men. Our King has commanded me to institute the Inquistion here in Naples."

Don Gaetano hesitatingly faced Don Pedro and replied.

"But, my Lord, the nobles are already showing unrest with us. Surely they will not accept...." His words trailed off as he was abruptly interrupted.

"Let me be the judge of what they will or will not accept.

We are in charge here, not them. What our king orders us to do is what will be done."

Don Gaetano knew that it was futile to argue with his superior. He was well aware of Don Pedro's ruthlessness in dealing with local problems having witnessed the summary public executions of petty thieves and miscreants who had disobeyed his decree against carrying concealed arms into the city at night.

"Then, my Lord, I will assist you in any way that I can to fulfill the wishes of his majesty."

Rumors of the Inquisition, however, were immediately greeted with protests that often turned violent, since landowners knew that even the innocent who were questioned often had their land holdings confiscated from them.

*

Maria suggested that she escort him on a tour of Naples and let him become acquainted with Campania and its various provinces before attempting to locate any relatives or at least families that bore the name Catalano.

"We'll start in Naples and then visit the surrounding areas of Campania so that you can better understand where your ancestors lived and perhaps the relationship, if any, between their homes and the port of Naples.

I think you did indicate that one of your ancestors left from there.

Do you know if he had any relatives in Naples?"

"Yes, my grandfather, Felix Catalano, left from Naples on a ship called the **Cheribon**...or at least I think he did. I have a document of his with that name stamped on it.

Strangely enough, I haven't been able to locate him on the Ellis Island website even though I'm sure that it sailed from Naples to New York."

"Many immigrants changed their names when they arrived in America…or had them changed by the authorities who had trouble pronouncing or spelling their names."

"I don't think that was the problem. As you can see, it's not a difficult name to pronounce or spell, and it seems to be fairly common on the Ellis Island website. All my relatives proudly bore the name *Catalano* including my mother."

"Well, suppose we worry about that later. Once we establish some facts about your ancestors here, hopefully we can settle the question about the name and where they sailed from…and on what ship.

And relatives in Naples?"

"I don't know of any relatives in or around Naples. The family never spoke of any."

"Now, when would you suggest we start your tour?"

"Since you're being so gracious in offering your time and expertise, I'm at your mercy.

Just name a time that's convenient for you."

"How about tomorrow morning?

I can pick you up around eight-thirty."

"That would be perfect."

"By the way, where are you staying?"

"Uh, I haven't quite worked that out yet."

"Then by all means, you'll stay with us. We have a spare bedroom and I won't take no for an answer.

In case you are not aware, there are no hotels here in Campagna."

Already succumbing to her good looks and overwhelmed by her kind offer, he couldn't possibly refuse.

"Done."

"Then let me close up here and we'll go to my place and get you situated before dinner. It's right behind the museum."

*

"You know, I never even asked if you were married," she asked as they walked the short distance from the museum to her dwelling.

"No, I'm not.

I came close a time or two, but always managed to escape." He smiled as he uttered the latter words in a hushed tone.

She laughed in response.

"I hope you don't think it too forward of me to offer to put you up in our home? After all, we've just met.

Although, I must confess that I feel as though I've known you for a long time."

She blushed.

"I'm sorry. That's not something I would usually say to a virtual stranger."

"No offense taken, Maria. I've had the same feeling about you since we met earlier today."

They stood there surveying one another for a few moments. Finally, she interrupted the silence.

"Well, here we are" she uttered as they made their way through the front doorway of the modest two story home.

"Well, let me show you to your room. I hope you don't mind the clutter, but since mother died, I haven't really felt like cleaning things out. It's very difficult to dispose of a loved one's possessions."

"You don't have to explain. I lost both of my parents in recent years. After mom went, it took me more than a year to clean out the house and ready it for sale. When someone finally bought it, I felt like I was being a traitor to my parents, even though I knew it was the right move and had to be done."

She stopped for a moment on the steps to the loft and put her hand on his forearm.

"Thank you for being so understanding."

The gaze in her eyes made him realize that this ostensibly chance meeting almost certainly had to have been preordained. He felt a warmth in her presence that he had never experienced with any other woman he had known...even those with whom he had been intimate.

She led him to the top of the steps and into a small room with a single bed that was piled high with her late mother's garments, an old shawl and several worn blankets. The furnishings were spartan.

The room appeared untouched, as though it had been ignored for quite a while. A small picture frame containing a single photo adorned the solitary piece of furniture.

He couldn't help but notice a thin layer of dust coating the surface of the nightstand as he picked it up.

"Your mother's picture?"

"Yes", was all she could muster in response.

"You look a lot like her.

She must have been beautiful in her youth."

Maria smiled but made no additional comments as she lovingly lifted the items off the bed.

"Let me take these into the hallway. There's a closet there that I can put them in."

Without hesitation, he instinctively grabbed some of the items on the bed and followed her to the hall closet.

"You're so very kind," she said.

Her words and the way in which they were spoken suggested a relationship that could easily become more than platonic.

*

"When you invited me to stay, you said *we* would be glad to have you. Who else lives here with you?"

He had just returned to the ground level living room after changing for dinner.

She cast a furtive glance at him.

"I hope you won't think me devious.

I can't break myself of the habit of using the pleural *we* since mother died. There is no one else here but me now. It's so very difficult to think of someone you've known your whole life in the past tense.

Please forgive me."

Whatever her excuse, he found it exciting being alone in her presence. Not a suspicious person by nature, he hadn't considered the invitation to be anything but a kind gesture by a stranger.

"Not at all. I understand fully.

As I mentioned earlier, I lost both my parents fairly recently. I live alone too, except for a few pets.

I have to admit, I sometimes find myself referring to *we* or *us*, meaning me and the pets."

"You haven't told me where home is?"

"I've lived in a suburb of Atlanta, Georgia for the past ten years. Growing up, we moved to many places since my father was a professional soldier."

"What is this word…suburb?"

"It's a town on the edge of a larger city. There are dozens of them that make up what we refer to as the Atlanta metropolitan area."

"Ah! Sobborgo.

That's how we pronounce it in Italian.

"Sobborgo", he repeated.

"Molto bene…very good. You have an ear for pronouncing things correctly in my language."

"I attended a few conversational Italian classes before embarking on this trip. I figured it would be useful. I've been advised numerous times that people in foreign countries are generally more helpful if you at least make an effort to speak their language. But I can see already that I should have attended more."

He reached into his coat pocket and fished out his copy of **Spoken Italian Made Easy** and held it up for her to see.

"I find these kinds of books helpful, but there's nothing like spending time in the country whose language you want to learn… and especially when in the company of someone from that country who speaks the language fluently."

She smiled again in return.

He wasn't ready to conclude that her words and actions were a direct invitation to an affair or just the beginning of an association that eventually could lead to more than just a business transaction.

But he was willing to find out!

*

"We don't have many places to eat here in Campagna, but we can drive to Eboli…it's only about eight kilometers. There's a wonderful local restaurant there that I visit whenever I can. They make all their pastas and sauces themselves."

"I came through there on the way to Campagna. As you know, it's the only way to get here.

By the way, it was my grandmother's home town. I learned a fair amount about it from the internet and maps.

But Campagna!

It was just a dot on the internet world atlases. I was just lucky that I saw the sign pointing to it as I was driving through Eboli.

You're in charge, so lead the way."

She had a Fiat Coupe parked behind the house in a garage situated midway between it and the museum.

"I'm lucky to have a garage. They're not common here and generally very expensive. But, it helps protect the car from the elements and the thieves who would love to steal it. Fiat is the most commonly stolen car in my country."

"So I've been told.

I had requested one from the rental car agency at the Rome airport, but they wouldn't let me bring one anywhere near Naples... for the reason you just mentioned."

*

Pasquales... the restaurant she had referred to in Eboli...was small and quaint. The dining area consisted of a single rectangular room divided evenly by about a dozen tables. Each had a small wine bottle holding a candle and a vase with a single fresh flower situated on a checkered tablecloth of red, green and white...the colors of the Italian flag.

The kitchen was located to the rear of the dining area.

Inexpensive reproductions of famous Italian scenes such as the Roman coliseum, the Bay of Naples and the red rooftops of Florence adorned the walls.

"This place reminds me of a restaurant I used to frequent in Philadelphia, although I'm sure the food will be better here.

I know the company will be."

Maria put her hand on his.

"You are so sweet.

What were you doing in Philadelphia?

I thought you told me you lived in Atlanta?"

Not wanting to reveal too much about himself just yet, he kept his answer short.

"I had some relatives there that I visited whenever I was nearby. My cousin's husband owned the restaurant that I was referring to...called Mi Famiglia. It was located in the northern suburbs... Sobborgo...of Philadelphia just off Roosevelt Boulevard.

Unfortunately, my relatives are all gone now.

Have you ever been to Philadelphia?"

"No.

Unfortunately, I have not had the pleasure to go to America... yet. But I certainly plan to one day. Right now, I need to get my affairs settled here and decide what I'm going to do with the rest of my life...and where.

Perhaps I'll consider a trip to America before I start a new job...."

He cut her off in midsentence.

"You'd be more than welcome in Atlanta. There are many things to see and do in our fair city. I believe you'd find Georgia as hospitable as I'm finding Italy. And I know you'd enjoy our famous port city, Savannah and our neighboring state's main attraction... Hilton Head Island, South Carolina."

He could see that she was considering this an invitation to visit.

"Perhaps we can discuss that later. It all sounds so very enticing. I've seen articles about those places in travel magazines and they all look very exciting.

Now, I'm famished! What would you like to eat?"

"Why don't you order for the two of us?"

*

The distaste of the Inquisition by the local populace of Naples, coupled with their resentment over the closing of "academies" or discussion groups, forced Charles V to reconsider his methods of governing. In an effort to calm the citizenry, he decided by 1552 to transfer Don Pedro to Siena since his continued presence in Naples would only have served to continue infuriating his subjects.

Not knowing that their decades of friendship would end the following year with the death of Don Pedro, due to heart failure while visiting nearby Florence, Don Gaetano Catalano instead escaped to Catanzaro in the Calabria region where he set out to establish his own life and legacy apart from the Spanish nobleman with whom he had been associated since childhood.

CHAPTER FOUR

Pasquales was all that she had promised and more. Maria ordered a variety of antipasti and entrees, all of which were exceptional. But it was being in the company of this beautiful and intriguing woman that excited him the most.

It was hard to fathom that only yesterday he was in Atlanta, and that he had known Maria Rosato for only a part of one day. Though he had slept only briefly on the flight to Rome, he wasn't the least bit tired as he sat and listened to her relate portions of her life story to him. It was as if time had stood still since he entered the small museum in Campagna and first set eyes on this lovely creature now sitting opposite him in of all places... his grandmother's hometown.

While she had mentioned that she was a widow when they first conversed at the museum, she had not added any details.

He was reluctant to enquire about the circumstances.

As the dishes were being cleared from the table, Maria positioned her hand on his. Gazing across the table at him, she suddenly began telling him additional details about her past.

"You don't have to be afraid to ask about my late husband. It's been almost three years since I lost him.

Paulo was my first and only true love. We met in Naples and wed after only three months dating. He owned a bookstore that specialized in rare manuscripts. We worked together until...." She abruptly burst into tears.

"I'm so embarrassed."

He reached into his coat pocket and brought out a handkerchief. "Please...take it."

She accepted the white cloth and wiped the tears. He sat silently with concern showing on his face. After a few silent moments Maria continued.

"He was my whole life and then...just like that he was gone at age thirty-four. The doctors said it was some kind of congenital heart defect that led to a heart attack. It happened while he was driving. The car struck a bridge pillar and it was over in an instant."

He measured the distress on her face, then squeezed her hand to silently console her.

"Perhaps we should go back to your place?"

"Yes. I'd like that...especially since you'll be there. I've always hated being alone...I mean mother was family but it's different after you've had a man in your life."

"Even though I haven't been married, I have had a few close relationships and I know how I felt right after the breakup.

Things just didn't seem the same for quite a while afterwards."

He put his arm around her shoulder and pulled her close as they exited the restaurant and walked slowly to the car.

"Would you prefer that I drove?"

"Yes, thank you."

A brief twenty minutes later, they were back in Campagna, the car had been secured for the night in the garage and they had made it to the front door.

"Are you sure that you want me to stay here tonight?"

"More than ever.

We have a big day ahead of us tomorrow."

He had virtually forgotten her promise to show him around Naples and the Campania region. He suddenly realized how tired he was as he reviewed the day's events in his mind.

"Then I guess I should go up to my room and just say 'I'll see you in the morning'?"

'That would probably be best."

She leaned forward and kissed him on the cheek.

"Thank you for being so kind and understanding."

Spurred on by her affectionate gesture, he threw caution to the wind, pulled her close and kissed her passionately.

"I don't know what's come over me. I've never done anything quite that impulsive before."

"I like it.

Please don't stop. It's been a long time…too long."

She kissed him again and again, then took his hand and led him to her bedroom. Neither one slept much that night, nor the next day.

They didn't make it to Naples or anywhere else in Campania the following day. For the next twenty-four hours they never made it out of the house and barely out of the bedroom.

*

He was suddenly aware of the aroma of coffee and the sound of something sizzling on the stove.

"Good morning sleepyhead…I think that's the way you say it in your country. Would you like some breakfast?"

Before he could answer, she approached him with a cup of coffee in hand and greeted him with a kiss. He stared at the oversized glazed coffee mug and then at her as he accepted it with both hands.

"You know you need to be careful.

A guy could get used to all this affection and attention."

"Maybe that's what a girl is looking for…someone who needs and deserves all the special attention and affection that she has to give."

"Well, you certainly gave plenty of it to me in the past day and a half."

After throwing him a slightly embarrassed look, she quickly changed the subject.

"Would you like eggs with your breakfast sausage? I usually fry them completely, turn them over and then serve them with a little of my homemade pasta sauce."

"It's not what I would usually have in the morning, but it sounds great. I generally have cold cereal since it doesn't involve any talent to pour it from a package and add milk."

"You're so funny. I'd forgotten just how mornings could be with a man in my life.

I hope this hasn't all been too sudden for you?"

He hadn't really thought about it in that way. Somehow, even though only a day and a half had passed between them, he felt he had known her longer, and experienced deeper passion and more intense feelings about her than any woman he had been involved with romantically in the past.

He wasn't sure if she was looking for a commitment from him already...or just commenting on things that she was experiencing at that moment. He remembered his past liaisons and the feelings engendered...until his female companions began pressing him long before he felt it appropriate to be talking about engagement rings and wedding ceremonies...causing him to bolt from the relationship.

"No. Not at all.

I think you are the most special woman that I have ever met."

*

They finished breakfast in relative silence as each pondered the comments the other had offered.

"I think I have some good news for you" she suddenly exclaimed.

"I was up early and took the liberty to check a few things on the internet. I found out that the man that relative of yours worked for...Don Pedro of Toledo, mentioned in the letter from your Philadelphia great-uncle...is buried in Naples at the church of San Giacomo degli Spagnoli.

I though maybe we could go there later this morning...if you like? Of course, I don't know if it will help at all in finding anything about Don Gaetano."

A big smile broke out on his face.

"Where have you been all my life?

Of course I would like to go there."

She smiled and without any further conversation took him by the hand and led him back to the bedroom.

*

"It's a most impressive tomb. Did you ever think that one of your relatives worked for such an important man?"

"I've read this letter dozens of times and I never really gave much thought to Don Pedro of Toledo being of much real influence here in Naples. I realized that as Viceroy to a king that he was someone of stature…but I always imagined his fame residing more in Spain than here in Italy."

Maria stopped to read a plaque erected adjacent to the tomb.

"Did you know that Don Pedro's daughter, Elenora, married one of the Medicis?"

He rushed to her side to read the inscription.

"Elenora was married to Cosimo de Medici, son of Giovanni de Medici and Maria Salviati. She was born in 1522 and died in 1562.

Wow! She was only forty years old. I guess that was about average longevity in the sixteenth century come to think of it. But I thought from what I remember of Italian history that Cosimo de Medici lived in the fourteenth century."

"I think there's more here about the Medicis." She picked up a pamphlet from a box nearby that chronicled the history of the Medici family.

"Ah, you were correct…at least partly.

Cosimo de Medici, the elder, lived in the thirteen hundreds. He was the son of Giovanni, the founder of the Medici family, and brother of Lorenzo. Cosimo became head of a branch of the family known as the Cafaggiolo while Lorenzo was leader of the Popolani.

Cosimo's grandson was Lorenzo the Magnificent, the patron of many of Florence's famous citizens such as Michelangelo, Botticelli and Leonardo de Vinci. After his death, Charles V tried to take control of Florence by placing Alessandro as Duke of the city. Called 'Il Moro' because of his dark features and resembling the Moors, he ruled for only a short time until his assassination in 1537.

That's when the Cosimo de Medici, husband of Elenora, assumed leadership of the Popolani branch of the family which was then in control. He became an elder statesman after securing Florence from the Republic of Sienna in 1559. He instituted the building of new cities, promoted innovative farming techniques and advocated for the arts.

Elenora, disliked at first because of her Spanish heritage, eventually became endeared to the people of Tuscany for her patronage of the arts and promotion of the building of new churches and support of the Jesuit order in Florence."

"Wow! That's quite a legacy."

"Now, where does Don Gaetano fit into all of this?"

"I guess we'll have to keep searching for clues as to where he went. Perhaps some of the other stops I have planned will be more fruitful."

As they walked toward the parking area where they had left her Fiat, he saw a sign for Gelato.

"Shall we?"

"I love gelato. I hope you find Italian ice cream to your liking. Let me order for the two of us, if you don't mind?

Would you be so kind as to find us a table on the terrace?"

He only smiled in response and turned toward the terrace dining area. A young couple was just leaving so he quickly secured the only available picnic table with umbrella.

She returned a few moments later with two dishes of gelato handsomely decorated with cookies in the shape of the leaning tower of Pisa on one and the Duomo of Florence on the other.

"Your country truly is the place for artists," he remarked.

"Enjoy!"

CHAPTER FIVE

Don Gaetano Catalano was drawn to Catanzaro by the Spanish domination of the city and the region: Catanzaro was capital of both the province which bore the same name and the region of Calabria. In 1528, during the revolt of the Calabrian barons, Pedro Alarcon de Mendoza resisted a long siege and gained for the city the title of magnifica et fidelissima by Charles V, granting it the right to mint coins.

The city was originally founded in the tenth century by Byzantium, but soon conquered by Robert Guiscard, the Norman king. Like most of the other areas of Italy, it suffered the vicissitudes of being repeatedly conquered until finally it became part of the new kingdom of Italy in 1860.

The origins of the name, Catanzaro, remain obscure. Some believe it was a compilation of the names of two Byzantine generals, Kattaro and Zaro. Another theory says that Zaro was the original name of the river (Zarapotamo) and that the Greek words kata Zaro meant beyond the river. A third theory attributes the name to the Greek words kata antheros... "on the flowery hills".

The old town was built over three hills: St. Rocco hill, Episcopate's hill and St. John's hill and is split by the steep Fiumarella valley. Catanzaro lido, the beach town, lies about five kilometers south. It was often referred to as the city of the three V's from St. Vitaliano, its patron saint; velvets, being a textile center from Norman times, and venti, a reference to the winds that blew in from the Sila mountains and the sea.

*

Don Gaetano hand delivered the letter of introduction given him by Don Pedro to Pedro Alarcon de Mendoza's successor. Spanish domination of the region was already waning and Don Gaetano's reception was less cordial than he had expected.

In what would become a monumental decision made virtually on the spot, Don Gaetano elected to establish himself as a merchant in the city known as the silk producing capital of the world. The finest silk garments and lace were made and sold to merchants from around the major European cities at the province's main port, Reggio Calabria. And that city also provided these same goods directly to the finest world courts and to the Vatican.

*

He was approaching forty-five, elderly by the standards of the day since the average life span was only a few years beyond that. The shop he had created the preceding year was already doing very well thanks to his reputation for honest dealing, timely delivery of goods and services promised, and fair pricing of his merchandise. He was pleased when one of his customers approached him at home with an offer that once again would have repercussions across the ensuing centuries.

"Don Gaetano, I would like you to meet my daughter, Margherite."

Don Juan de Salas was many years his elder and his daughter was approaching thirty years of age and still unwed.

"You do me honor to bring such a beautiful young lady to my humble home. How may I be of service, Don Juan?"

"Margherite is my last unmarried daughter and you would honor me to accept her hand in marriage. She will make a wonderful wife and I believe an equally fit mother. I have a dwelling in the mountains near here that I would be pleased to offer as a dowry."

Don Gaetano considered the offer carefully. Margherite twirled in full view of him at her father's request, then shyly stole away to the corner of the room. He was enamored by her angelic face, long auburn tresses and curvaceous body.

"We have discussed it already at home. My wife and daughter both agree that you would make a fit husband for her. I could not be more proud than to bestow my blessing on such a union.

But perhaps you need more time. I know that this is all very sudden...."

"No!

I need no more time.

Margherite is a beautiful young woman and you, Don Juan are a reputable man and a good friend. I believe that she will be more than suitable as my wife.

Therefore, I will accept your offer.

Now, let us discuss the terms over a glass of wine."

Don Juan instructed Margherite to deliver the good news to her mother and tell her that they could begin preparations for the upcoming nuptials.

"Now, Don Gaetano, about that dwelling. Perhaps you would like to see it?"

*

The hills northwest of Catanzaro were steep and foreboding in places. Five or six kilometers set amidst the rugged topography of Calabria was a full half day's journey for the pair as they made their way on foot. Don Gaetano carried a curved walking stick fashioned from an old barrel stave. Don Juan similarly carried an old shepherd's crook to assist in the long climb.

"Don Juan, we are getting to be old men when we find ourselves struggling to climb these foothills.

Perhaps a short break?"

Don Juan was more than happy to accommodate Don Gaetano. Despite having made the trek from Catanzaro to Gagliano many times, he relished the opportunity to stop for a rest and gaze at the scenery.

"The hills here are some of Calabria's finest. And the view is magnificent. One can see the city established on both sides of the Fiumarella Valley all the way to the lido."

They sat quietly for a short while as they sought to regain their stamina.

"Let us be off, my friend. We have only a short distance remaining and we should plan to be home before dark as the footing is treacherous in the dim light of dusk or the dark of night."

"Yes" replied Don Gaetano.

*

Gagliano was a tiny village of only several hundred people, most of whom engaged in farming. Though its elevation was similar to that of Catanzaro, it had the advantage of being more central in the province and overall was more temperate and had fewer problems from the wind. Balmy breezes from the Ionian Sea were welcome during the spring and summer; at other times of the year they often became gale force winds that plagued the cities closer to the coast.

Finally, after another half hour's walk, they approached their destination.

"Don Gaetano, this is my humble home that I offer to you as a gift for accepting the hand of my daughter. I know that you will make her happy as you and she have made me happy by agreeing to this match."

The structure was small and in the ancient Roman style. Its notable exception was a ***peristylium*** or colonnaded garden that was open on the ocean side giving occupants an unobstructed view of Catanzaro and the Ionian seacoast in the distance.

"Don Juan, your abode is quite exquisite...perhaps too great a gift to me.

But...I accept.

I am sure that Margherite and I will gladly use it to escape from Catanzaro any time that we can. I am already busy grooming an apprentice to run my business for those times when I must be away...or choose to get away now that I will have an excuse to do so."

He smiled at Don Juan who quickly discerned his meaning.

"One can never have too many grandchildren," he replied.

*

The wedding that took place on June 5, 1555 was spectacularly simple. Margherite was beautiful in a gown of light blue silk brocade with red and green crosses emblazoned on the large sleeves. Her auburn hair was long and flowing, reaching to just below her shoulders.

The church of Sant'Omobono, built in the twelfth century, was chosen for the ceremony. Most of the townspeople attended the affair presided over by the church's vicar. Simple gold rings bearing the inscription Amor Vincit Omnia (love conquers all) were exchanged, and small silk pouches containing a single gold coin from the local mint were given to each guest. The wedding feast that followed continued for several days in keeping with the dictates of the period. However, Don Gaetano and his bride stole away during the night of the first day and made their way to their retreat home in Gagliano, to consummate their wedding.

Two months later, Margherite announced that she was with child...the first of seven that would bless their union.

CHAPTER SIX

"You know, that business of one of Don Pedro of Toledo's daughters being married to a Medici continues to intrigue me. Maybe we should go to Florence and see if we can come up with something to connect them to Don Gaetano."

"I suppose it's worth a trip there, even though it's what you would say is...a long shoot?"

He laughed loud and long.

Sensing that she was hurt by his reaction to her misuse of an English slang term, he took her hand, kissed it and then gently corrected her.

"A long shot", he replied.

"Well, I was close.

Anyway, you need to see Firenze.

Tuscany is certainly one of the most scenic parts of Italy...next to Campania, of course!

You'll love the countryside and the cities and the art museums. Of course, we'll need to spend several days.

I know a perfect small town villa nearby that rents rooms and provides wonderful Italian dishes and homemade wine. It's been one of my favorite places to stay and it will be even more special in your company."

The way she gazed at him and the inflection in her voice said it all.

"How can a fella resist such an offer?

You're right...I do need to see Tuscany and Firenze. I'm not sure that I have any relatives there or that we'll find anything that relates my family to the Medicis...but heck, we'll have a good time anyway.

But you know, I've been thinking about something else.
Have you ever been to Spain?"

"Just to Barcelona several years ago with my husband on a two day business trip. So we didn't really see much of the country.

Why? What did you have in mind?"

"Well, we keep mentioning Toledo. I wonder if we could learn anything there about Don Pedro or his family? Why don't we fly to Madrid and drive down to Toledo? I'll have to check a map, but I think it's just a short distance south of Madrid."

"That seems like a good idea before we start looking here in Italy" she responded.

"When do you think you can get away?"

"I need to tell the museum that I'll be taking a leave of absence... or perhaps just resign. They're not that busy anyway so I think they'll get along just fine without me."

"Well, I know someone that can't."

She smiled and accepted his response as a good omen. Their relationship, although brief, had been intensely gratifying and all signs pointed to a happy conclusion.

"I'll check on flights out of Naples or Rome and we can plan accordingly after you check with the museum in the morning."

"Perfect"

*

He awoke to the sound of a door opening and closing.

"Buongiorno" she said as she opened the leather curtains, exposing the windows and allowing the bright sun to illuminate the bedroom.

Maria was already dressed and held a cup of hot coffee in her hand.

"Buongiorno to you, too" he replied as she kissed him lightly on the lips and then handed him the mug of coffee.

"Are you heading to the museum?"

She showed him her wristwatch.

"Twelve o'clock noon?

Why I couldn't possibly have slept that late!"

Maria laughed.

"Well, you did.

I didn't want to disturb you so I got up and dressed and went to the museum. I decided to resign so that we'll be free to do all the research necessary to find the answers about your family.

So...you can go ahead and arrange for our trip to Spain."

*

"I checked on flights from Naples and Rome and I think the only real option is Rome. All the Naples flights require major layovers, mostly in Rome. We can fly non-stop from Rome to Madrid on Iberia Airlines for under $300 each.

How about we drive to Rome tomorrow and fly to Madrid the following day? The flight leaves at 12 noon. I'll see if I can get us a room at one of the hotels near the airport."

"That sounds wonderful. I'm sure we can find something to do here today and then maybe drive to Eboli for dinner at Pasquales."

"No argument from me."

*

Late morning the following day, the couple was en route to Rome in her Fiat. He had secured a room at the Hilton hotel on the grounds of Leonardo da Vinci airport, better known as Fiumicino because of its proximity to the small coastal town.

They bypassed Naples and headed straight for Rome, arriving at the Hilton just before four p.m.

"What a marvelous day for traveling" Maria noted." The weather had been perfect at sixty degrees with blue skies.

"I would suggest we get settled here and have dinner in one of the hotel restaurants. I've had enough driving for one day" she added.

He nodded his agreement.

*

By nine-thirty a.m. the following morning, they were up, had eaten breakfast and were on the hotel shuttle to the airport for their noon flight to Madrid.

"It's been quite a while since I've been on a flight. How long is it?" she asked.

"About two and a half hours.

You're not nervous are you?"

"Not now. Not when I'm with you." She nuzzled against his shoulder.

*

By two-thirty, Iberia flight 3231 was taxiing into terminal four at Madrid's Barajas airport. They quickly secured their baggage, bypassed passport control since they were in the Schengen area (a passport free area in Europe) and proceeded to their rental car pickup kiosk.

Within thirty minutes they were on the M-50 bypass, heading south towards Toledo.

"I hope this isn't a wild goose chase" he muttered.

He turned towards Maria only to see that confused look on her face once again.

"It means I hope we are not wasting our time."

She smiled.

*

"What is that song you're humming?"

"Are you familiar with the play and movie called 'Man of LaMancha'?"

"I've heard of it but I don't really know it" Maria replied.

"We just passed a sign saying we are in the province of Castile-LaMancha. Toledo is the capital city.

Somehow I'm sort of expecting to see Don Quixote or Sancho Panza come riding out of the hills. And windmills…where are the windmills?"

Maria was as confused as she had ever been and the expression on her face reflected it.

He laughed, realizing her befuddlement.

"They are two of the main characters in the play. It's based on a novel by Miguel Cervantes about an elderly wandering knight errant who is 'tilting at windmills' as the story is told.

I was humming 'The Impossible Dream'. It's the principal song from the play."

"Can you sing it for me? The melody sounded nice."

"I'll try. But as they say: I'd better keep my day job. Here goes nothing.

> To dream the impossible dream
> To fight the unbeatable foe
> To bear with unbearable sorrow
> To run where the brave dare not go
> To right the unrightable wrong
> To love pure and chaste from afar
> To try when your arms are too weary
> To reach the unreachable star...

Well you get the drift I'm sure."

He glanced her way again and once more there was that look.

"The words are lovely but everything else you said confused me more. You have a lovely voice by the way."

He chose to ignore the praise. After a moment of silence, he pointed into the distance.

"That's Toledo up on the hill. The building on the summit is the Alcazar."

"How do you know so much about a country you've never visited?" she queried.

He pointed to his cell phone.

"Wonderful little device. And Google is a great app to have on your phone. You can find out about almost anything in a matter of minutes...as long as there is a cell tower nearby.

I'm going to drive around to the south of town first so that we can see the famous view of the city with the Tagus River partially surrounding it like a moat."

The view was spectacular just as it had been shown on numerous web sites he had visited. Finally, they entered the town and drove through the narrow old streets to the summit abutting the Alcazar.

"Well, here we are. It doesn't look as imposing standing next to it as it does from a distance."

Maria nodded her agreement.

"You know, my love, it's almost five-thirty. I say we call it a day and find a place to stay for the night, get some dinner and then some rest. It's been a long day. Besides, isn't it time that we didn't have a console between us?"

He looked down at the space between them in the car and immediately agreed, getting her meaning.

"My travel guide recommends the Parador de Toledo hotel. It's supposed to be quite elegant…and expensive. I hope they have a room available."

After stopping for directions, he found the hotel with a modicum of trouble.

"I'll be right back. Wish us luck."

She waited while he checked on room availability and was pleased to see him returning after only a short while.

"They had a last minute cancellation so I was able to get us a suite…at a price. But what the heck, it's only money and who knows if we'll ever get back here."

The room was spectacularly appointed with king size bed, a chaise lounge and overstuffed chair, Jacuzzi and wall mounted fifty inch television; and from the balcony that faced southwest, a view of the Tagus River.

"What a sunset. It looks like something you might expect to see in the movies." She moved toward his side and leaned in for a kiss.

"What about dinner? Should we go out or eat in the hotel restaurant?"

"Let's see if they have a menu here in the room. Perhaps that will help us decide."

He found one in the bedside table drawer.

"They seem to have a nice selection of Spanish dishes as well as standard fare such as steak and seafood. And they have a terrace that has a terrific view of the city according to this." He pointed to the pictures of the terrace dining on the menu cover.

*

"The paella was outstanding. I particularly enjoyed the chorizo and shrimp mixed with it. Usually I don't care for things mixed

together, but this was especially tasty. Perhaps it was the company…
and the Sangria…that made everything taste so good."

He eased her onto the bed, kissed her lips and agreed with her
every statement. The rest of the night took care of itself.

Early the next morning, he was up and bathing while she slept.
When he finished, he sat on the bedside and caressed her gently.

"Good morning, sleepyhead. Are you ready to get started on
our quest for information about Don Pedro?"

She fluttered her eyelids, still half asleep.

"Wouldn't you rather come back to bed for a while?" She put
her hand on his thigh and began creeping upward.

"Well!"

About forty-five minutes later, they were both up. Maria went
into the bathroom to begin her morning routine.

"Why don't you have some coffee sent to the room for me while
you get some breakfast. I might be a while."

"I'll just get coffee and rolls and worry about eating later. We
can find a local restaurant for lunch near the Alcazar. That's where
the main library is located."

About two hours later, they arrived at the library by taxi.

Their search was disheartening from the start. They found that
most of the locals were not fluent in English making it difficult
to get help with their project. When they finally did obtain some
information about Don Pedro, the only relationship they could
find to Toledo was his name. As it turned out, he had been born
near Salamanca, a community about one hundred miles from
Toledo. This all occurred in the sixteenth century before Spain
was the nation of today and while Toledo was the capital of Castile.
Valladolid and then Madrid subsequently became the capitals of
modern Spain.

"So, what do we do now" Maria asked.

"We could go to Salamanca…but I can't find much here about
Don Pedro and that city either.

So, as a compromise, why don't we go visit Granada and the
Alhambra? It's not too far from here and it's a place I always wanted
to visit. Again, I don't know if or when we would have another
chance to see that part of Spain."

"Didn't the Alhambra have something to do with the Moors?"

"I see you remember a little bit of history. Yes. It has been a fortress and palace for both Muslim and Christian religious leaders beginning in the ninth century. I don't really know much more of the details."

They left Toledo the following morning and arrived in Granada that afternoon. After securing a room at the Alhambra Palace hotel for two nights, they spent time in the city sightseeing, having arranged a walking tour of the Alhambra for the following morning.

"Well, that was quite a tour but now my feet are killing me" Maria said after the three hours of walking, most of which involved hills and staircases. "I think the Generalife gardens were as spectacular as the palace buildings themselves; I can certainly see why people want to come here."

"Let's just go back to the hotel. We can have drinks and snacks on the terrace and I need to arrange our flight back to Rome. I think it's time to resume our search in Florence. This was a nice side trip, but we didn't really learn anything significant about Don Pedro and nothing in our quest for information about Miguel Catalano."

The schedules for Iberia airlines indicated a non-stop flight from Madrid to Rome leaving at eleven-fifty-five.

"We'll have to get up early to make it. But I'm eager to get back to Italy. It arrives around two-thirty, so we can be in the Florence area by six o'clock."

"I'll call Villa il Calle. It's a small quaint hotel just outside Florence...the one I was referring to the other day before we decided to go to Spain. They usually can accommodate me there."

"Great."

CHAPTER SEVEN

The A1 traffic from Rome to Florence was moderately heavy during the late afternoon…at least by the standard that he was accustomed to around Atlanta. While he was used to speeds of up to seventy or eighty miles per hour around the Georgia capital, in Italy such speeds made him feel like he was standing still.

Maria elected to drive the Fiat, giving him the opportunity to examine the countryside in an unhurried manner and to observe some of the Italian driving customs that were previously unknown to him.

"Why are those cars behind us flashing their lights all the time?"

"Now it's my turn to laugh.

When they want to pass on the inside lane where passing is only permitted, they flash their lights to indicate that you must get out of the way…."

"Or else they will run you over." He finished the sentence for her.

"Already you can read my mind.

My husband used to do that too."

He didn't respond. He wasn't sure if comparison with former spouses, living or deceased was a good thing. He hadn't known her long enough to know her feelings in that regard.

"Well, what am I thinking now?" he asked coyly as he squeezed her right thigh.

"I'm thinking that you are a bad boy…but you don't have to stop if you don't want to." She put her hand on top of his and looked contentedly at him as they continued on towards Florence.

He didn't move his hand!

"Please be on the lookout for route SP1 as we approach Florence. That's where we exit to Bagno a Ripoli. It comes in on the east side of Florence. The place we'll be staying at is called Villa il Calle.

It's on Via Montisoni just off of SP1."

He continued to enjoy the countryside while she drove on quietly. It was almost an hour later that he yelled out.

"There.

The sign says SP1 two kilometers."

"It will be good to get to the hotel. Between flying and driving, it will have been a full day and I'm sure we'll both be very tired.

Perhaps a glass of wine and then we can get cozy?"

"You won't hear any objections from me."

*

The fifteen years immediately following the marriage of Don Gaetano and Margherite de Salas were productive both from the business and personal standpoints. Two of the seven children had succumbed to various "fever" illnesses prevalent at the time, but the other five...now ages four to fourteen were all healthy and progressing toward adulthood.

Then on June 23 of the year 1570, Don Gaetano suddenly died. He had complained of feeling tired most of the time. In the months prior to his death, climbing the hills in and around Catanzaro and Gagliano in particular had become more troublesome, significantly affecting his breathing.

Margherite was unsure what to do at first. Her father had died some seven years earlier and her mother the year before. She now was faced with the task of raising five children, none of whom had reached their majority yet.

Miguel, the oldest, who rightfully would inherit his father's title and wealth, assured his mother that together they should continue the business. He felt confident that he had learned the trade sufficiently from his father and could be trusted to run it with his mother's help.

Antonio, who was twelve, conveyed his disagreement of Miguel's optimism to his mother.

Despite his younger age, he was far more astute in business matters than his brother, and did not trust Miguel to assume control of his father's trade since he lacked the personal skills that had made it a success for their father.

The other three children...Teresa, Maria and Vito...were ages four to nine and had no valid opinions to offer on the dilemma.

Margherite would have preferred that Antonio were in line to assume control of her late husbands affairs, but acquiesced to the line of succession.

The next eight years saw the gradual diminishment of the silk and fabric trade from Catanzaro as merchants closer to Rome and the major cities of Europe became better established and were able to deliver the goods directly to their customers sooner and at lower prices.

Antonio, now twenty, had been at odds with his brother ever since their father's death; but being the non-inheriting son, he had been unable to deter Miguel from adopting numerous unscrupulous practices that were now causing the business to falter.

So it was with a heavy heart that Antonio approached his mother and announced that he was leaving home to find his own fortunes. He felt he could no longer live in the shadow of Miguel.

"My son, we will all miss you dearly...but I understand you must have a life of your own.

Where will you go?"

Already tears were running down her cheek.

"I don't know. I'm going to travel west but I hope to stay in Calabria if I can find work and a place to live. Hopefully I can find someone who can use my skills as a gamer."

"Yes. I believe that would suit you well.

Your father and I always admired your ability to work with birds and animals. Perhaps that is what you are destined to do.

But you must let me know where you are and how you are doing. You must stay in touch with us...." Unable to finish the thought, she just pulled him close to her and held him tightly.

"When will you leave?"

"In the morning."

There was nothing more to be said, only silent thoughts of their futures without one other.

*

Antonio had been but a few weeks away from home when fate led him to Monteleone, a small village near the Gulf of Sant'Eufemia on the Tyrrhenian Sea. Like most Italian cities of antiquity, it had gone through various periods of domination by local tribes like the Brutti, a Greek tribe that occupied the *toe* of Italy until defeated by Rome in the 3rd century B.C.; then the Carthaginians; and finally the Romans again. After the fall of Rome in the fifth century, it remained at relative peace for several hundred years. But because it occupied a strategic point (an ancient Greek acropolis), it was fought over by the Spanish, the Saracen Moors, and finally the Normans who built a castle over the remains of the Greek acropolis.

*

"Perhaps I can use your skills. Tell me about your experiences with birds and animals."

Antonio had secured a small room in the hill town of Monteleone and was fortunate to be directed to one of its leading citizens by the owner of the dwelling. And with those opening remarks, a long and lasting relationship was begun between Antonio Catalano and Luigi Cantrone.

"I have no formal training, but I have always had a way with animals and birds of all varieties. And I have worked hard to teach myself the art of falconry."

"Then by all means, Antonio, I am sure I can use you. I have had a long interest in falconry myself. Frederick II, a Norman king who was interested in falconry, rebuilt this city on the site destroyed by the Saracens in the ninth century and renamed it Monteleone, the mount of the lion.

You can begin as my apprentice. And, if you can prove your worthiness, I will see to it that you are named *capo guardacaccia* (chief gamekeeper) for the city."

"I will not let you down," Antonio replied.

CHAPTER EIGHT

Villa il Calle was a pleasant surprise to say the least. The description by Maria of "a small villa that rents rooms" hardly did it justice. In fact, it was a five star resort that just happened to have been a villa in years past. The original owners had passed on and the children who had inherited it were quick to accept an offer for purchase from one of Europe's leading hotel chains. Its proximity to Florence combined with its rural ambience made it a perfect site for those visiting the city but who preferred a more leisurely place to relax at day's end.

"Ah! Signorina Rosato. Buona sera.

It's so nice to see you again."

"Signore Abruzzi, it has been too long. We are here hoping to find some of my friend's ancestors and to do some research on the Medicis." Maria made introductions all around.

"Well, you have certainly come to the right place.

I have your special suite reserved for you as you requested. Also, I had my staff place a bottle of champagne on ice along with two glasses in your room...compliments of the house for a very special guest.

Will you be wanting dinner in your suite?"

"No. I think we would prefer a table a little later. Shall we say nine o'clock?

And thank you for the champagne...although it wasn't necessary."

"Signorina, it is my pleasure as always.

I will have your favorite table waiting for you.

Now, let me show you to your suite."

*

The suite was comprised of two fairly large rooms with a small connecting hallway from which the bathroom door exited.

The larger of the two rooms held a loveseat, two overstuffed recliners, several end tables with lamps, a coffee table and a large flat screen television. There was also a sink and countertop that held a coffee maker and a microwave oven. Below the oven was a small refrigerator.

Situated on the countertop was a bucket of ice that held the now chilled champagne. Next to the bucket were two Austrian crystal wine glasses, one green and the other rose colored.

The adjacent room had one king sized bed, unusual for most European hotels.

"Well, to say that I'm impressed would be an understatement. I assume that you must have stayed here fairly often?"

She hesitated briefly.

"Paulo…my late husband…as I told you dealt in rare manuscripts. We came to Florence quite often on business and always stayed here on those occasions. I failed to mention that some of the manuscripts that he dealt with were extremely rare and worth a great deal of money. He dealt with clients from around the world…."

She began to shed a tear and stopped mid-sentence.

He stayed silent for a few moments, then stepped forward with his handkerchief and dried her face.

"Why don't you get comfortable while I open the champagne? We have about two hours before dinner."

"Thank you. I'll be right back."

She returned momentarily in a robe and slippers.

He stood with the two wine glasses now full and offered her the rose colored one.

"Salut. The color of your glass reminds me that you are as lovely as a rose petal in bloom."

The tips of their glasses touched.

"What a romantic thing to say."

She tasted the champagne and then set the glass on the coffee table. As she spun back towards him, she opened her robe revealing her nakedness underneath. His eyes focused on her perfect breasts.

"Now that's what I call *the* ideal champagne toast.

I think…no…I know I'm going to enjoy Tuscany."

*

The almost two hours they had lain together had been but a tick of the clock. Maria rose from her slumber, sat on the bedside and looked at the bedside timepiece.

"It's a quarter to nine."

He responded with a moan, then turned toward her and kissed her on the lips.

"This has got to be a fantasy. Just a few days ago I was a lonely man from Georgia in search of my past and now all I can think about is my future. You've transformed my life."

"And you mine." She returned the kiss.

"And now my American friend, I'm famished. Signore Abruzzi will be expecting us."

*

The antipasti were fried calamari served with a dipping sauce of garlic tomato, and porcini dusted scallops with tomato relish. Maria chose one of the house original varietal wines bottled under the Villa il Calle label.

There followed a succession of courses including Caesar salad, the house special soup, Tuscan country bean, served with a variety of breads; and then the entrée of beef *braciole* served with risotto Milanese. Maria chose a burgundy to complement the beef.

"My goodness, I'm not accustomed to eating so much at one time. How do Italians keep from gaining weight if you eat like this every day?" he retorted.

"I think the secret is in the olive oil" she said with utter sincerity. He wasn't sure if she was being facetious or not.

Just when he thought that it was time for dessert, a large platter of pappardelle with mushroom Marsala sauce was placed in the center of the table, still replete with only partially eaten earlier offerings.

"You know I've dined in numerous authentic Italian restaurants back home, and I always forget about them serving pasta as the last dish. Perhaps we could entertain a 'doggy bag'?"

She only laughed in response.

"Mangia tutto...eat up. It's good for you."

Dinner was followed by espresso and Tiramisu.

"Would you like a little Galliano for an aperitif? They say it has an aphrodisiac effect."

"Just gazing at you is enough of an aphrodisiac for me.

But, if you will join me, I would love some?"

"You are so dolce...so sweet."

The maitre d' poured the golden liquid into small crystal aperitif glasses.

"Salut" he offered once again.

They sat gazing at one another for a few moments as they savored the liquor.

"Perhaps it is time to return to our room? We need to make plans for tomorrow."

Somehow the night disappeared without any thought about the next day...only the moment at hand.

*

"Let's begin with the Uffizi Museum" Maria suggested.

"We can visit part of it this afternoon and then return tomorrow and see the sections we miss today."

Their morning had segued into almost noon by the time the couple had done their respective routines following a wakeup love making session.

Coffee and a few light breakfast items had been delivered to the room at ten. He had quickly showered and dressed and sat patiently reading one of the morning English newspapers sent on the tray while Maria prepared herself in typical slow womanly fashion.

"I hope I haven't kept you waiting too long?"

One look at her made him forget any minor annoyance he might have felt, not being accustomed to waiting for anyone.

She was dressed in a two piece pant suit of rich Italian silk. The trousers were off white and the jacket a subdued red. Her blouse was ecru with a saffron scarf tucked below the collar of the jacket.

"I'm sorry. I didn't know I was to wear my *Esquire* outfit this morning."

She immediately caught his meaning and smiled.

"I mean, you look beautiful...like a page out of a fashion magazine" he quickly added.

"Thank you.

And you are quite handsome yourself."

He had chosen khaki trousers, and a light blue dress shirt accented by a dark blue blazer.

"So.

The Uffizi it is."

"I think it best that we take a taxi. It's a bit pricey, but parking is such a problem in the city."

"You're the expert."

She placed a call to the hotel concierge and a car was waiting by the time they reached the lobby.

"I'm sure you'll enjoy the city. And perhaps we'll get lucky and find some clues to your ancestors."

*

The SP1 that had taken them to Ville il Calle continued westward toward the old section of Firenze, connecting to Viale Donato Giannotti. After they had crossed the Arno River, it seemed to him that they took a thousand twists and turns before Maria finally announced "here we are."

He looked out the taxi window to see the edifice called the Uffizi museum.

After paying the taxi driver and the entrance fees to the museum, they proceeded to the main vestibule that had directions to the various historical periods represented, as well as featured artists and special exhibits.

"Why don't we start by reading a little about the museums history? I'm sure they have brochures that detail that here."

*

"It says here that the Uffizi was begun in 1560 by the architect Giorgio Vasari during the period when Cosimo de Medici I was consolidating his power in Florence. Designed and built in the shape of a horseshoe, it extends from the Piazza della Signoria to the Arno River where it connects by a bridge, the Ponte Vecchio, to the Palazzo. The original intent of the building was to house the offices (Uffizi) of the Grand Duchy. The last heir of the Medicis, Anna Maria Luisa, gave the several centuries of art collected by the Medicis, along with the buildings, to the city of Florence in 1737.

Do you recall who Cosimo I was married to?"

He pondered the question for a few moments.

"Elenora, daughter of Don Pedro of Toledo!"

Cosimo I. de' Medici (1519-1574), Grand Duke of Tuscany   Eleonora of Toledo

He reached over and gave her a big hug.

"I don't know if it means a thing about your ancestor, Don Gaetano Catalano, but already I feel connected to this place and I'm not even a relative", she said with great enthusiasm.

"I'm sure there must be more information here about the Medicis and their connections to occupy us for a considerable amount of time...we just need to start searching."

CHAPTER NINE

The sixteenth century was coming to an end and Antonio Catalano had been forced to make a decision.

Life in Monteleone had been good to him. He had indeed earned the title of *capo guardacaccia* and had held it for over thirty years. He had also earned the favor of the town, the region of Calabria and was known even to the heads of several other principalities and to the reigning pontiff of Rome himself, Clement VIII, the former Ippolito Aldobrandini, thanks to his knowledge and expertise of falconry.

He had been introduced to the pontiff by Alessandro de Medici, who would become Pope Leo XI on the death of Clement and unfortunately, die only twenty-seven days later and have one of the shortest pontificates in history.

Antonio had met Carmela Malpezzi soon after relocating to Monteleone. She was the daughter of a close friend of his mentor, Luigi Cantrone. The couple had married two years later and subsequently produced six children. The eldest, Francesco, had been sent to Florence as an apprentice in the house of Ferdinando de Medici.

Antonio had become a widower in 1595 with the premature death of Carmela who succumbed along with several of their children in all probability to a form of plague that swept through Italy during the last decade of the sixteenth century. Now with his health failing as well, Antonio elected to relocate to Tuscany to spend his remaining time with his son, Francesco.

Antonio managed to survive another four years, and then succumbed to heart failure as the century was coming to a close.

Meanwhile, Francesco found the justice system not to his liking and had transferred his interests to banking, another key profession of the Medici.

Following his father's death, he elected to relocate to the Campania region to seek his own fortune away from the domination of his mentors, the Medici. It was in the small town of Campagna, in Salerno province, that he would settle and become the progenitor of a family that would remain ensconced there until events drove his descendants Michele and Felice Catalano to America in the late nineteenth century.

*

"Unbelievable" was all he could say...and kept repeating over and over again as he and Maria traversed the halls and galleries of the Uffizi.

Each room of the Uffizi was like a separate art museum. Michelangelo, Rafael, DaVinci, Botticelli...all under the same roof. And just when he didn't think it possible to equal any of these giants of art, there came a room filled with Rembrandts and other Flemish artists of the 17th century.

"Unbelievable" was all he could utter once more.

"I take it you're finding this place to your liking?" Maria queried him jokingly, "but I think it best that we save some other parts of this landmark for another day...like the Palazzo Pitti and the Boboli Gardens just across the Ponte Vecchio."

He looked at her quizzically. He had heard the names before but wasn't sure what exactly those sites held.

"We've been at this for almost six hours and my feet are quite tired. Why don't we grab a cab back to the hotel and resume our quest for more clues about your ancestors here tomorrow?"

They had stopped briefly for espresso at one of the galleries' coffee kiosks and browsed the gift shop near the entrance foyer of the Uffizi. Otherwise, it had been non-stop viewing of art works of the masters.

He quickly agreed.

"You don't have to convince me. I'm not used to being up on my feet all day back home in Georgia. I could stand to put them up for a while...maybe even soak them.

And then some drinks and dinner would certainly be a glorious way to end a perfect day spent with my favorite lady in what undoubtedly has already become one of my favorite cities.

It really is grand.

Firenze...amore!"

"Well, I guess you were paying attention to things Italian after all. I love it too."

She took his arm and smiled, signaling her pleasure at his words as they made their way to the exit.

The attendant kindly secured a cab for them.

As they wound their way to Ville il Calle, she placed her head on his shoulder.

"I don't know what I would have done if you hadn't come along when you did. My life was so empty and I was so insecure about going back to Naples or Rome. I just wasn't sure what I wanted to do with the rest of my life."

"And you are now?" he asked somewhat hesitatingly.

"I think so.

And what about you?

Do you know what you want to do?"

He knew the minute the question left his lips that she would surely answer his question with a question...the old Socratic way.

He just smiled and held her closer to him.

She took this as a good sign although she would have preferred a positive verbal response.

*

Bright and early the following morning, the couple taxied back to the center of Florence for another day of sightseeing and hopefully a day of finding some clues to the Catalano connection to the Medici.

"This is the Palazzo Pitti...isn't it remarkable?" Maria queried as the taxi stopped in front of the entrance just across the River Arno from the Uffizi.

She chauffeured him through the front entrance where a wall mount held a map of the palace along with names of its component buildings and grounds. Several brochures detailing the contents of the various parts were held in a small stand next to the wall mount.

"It says here that the palazzo was originally commissioned by Luca Pitti, a prominent Florentine banker of the fifteenth century. It came to be the residence of the Medici family in 1549 when it was acquired from Buonaccorso Pitti, a descendant of Luca Pitti, by...Eleonora of Toledo, wife of Cosimo I de Medici.

There's another connection to her!"

She had his undivided attention.

"Read on."

"She employed Vasari, the same architect/painter that was responsible to a large degree for the Uffizi and who did frescoes in the cupola of the Duomo, to enlarge and enhance the palace. It had been quite foreboding and dark prior to his expansion and improvements.

He also built an addition, now known as the Vasari corridor, which connects the palace with the Ponte Vecchio across the Arno to the Uffizi. And he acquired land on the Boboli hill behind the palace that was turned into a large park and gardens now known as the Boboli Gardens."

"What's a Duomo?"

Maria turned toward him and laughed.

"Silly! I thought you did a little studying about Italy before you came here on your trip.

It's a cathedral.

Here in Florence it's the large church with the dome top done in red tile that dominates every picture you see of the old city. I'm sure you must have seen photos of it."

He smiled in return.

"Yes. I just didn't know what it was called in Italian.

Shall we start our tour of the palace?"

"Yes. I think we've read enough for now. We can read about the different areas as we come to them."

*

"Where would you like to begin?" Maria asked.

"I guess the old saying is 'begin at the beginning.'"

They were standing at the entrance to the Palatine gallery.

"This looks like an interesting room." They gazed at the myriad of portraits visible from the entrance portal.

"It says here in the guide book that this gallery houses over five hundred renderings mostly from the Renaissance period and that they were all part of the Medici and their successor's private collections. They are displayed now much the way they were in the time of the Medici...made to fit each room or wall and not in any particular order such as alphabetical or by periods or artists."

The couple wandered and observed and read about many of the paintings, paying particular attention to the portraits of many of the early Medici family members.

The gallery segued into the Royal apartments, a collection of fourteen smaller, more intimate rooms used by the Medici family and their successors...and most recently by the kings of Italy after the Risorgimento and up until the nineteen twenties.

"The palace was already a museum except for those rooms. They were converted to the Museum of Modern Art at that time," Maria commented.

"Look, here are portraits of Cosimo I di Medici and Eleonora of Toledo."

"Amazing!

Imagine! My family actually has a direct connection to these people who lived in the sixteenth century."

Maria looked closely at the paintings and the small plaques along side them that detailed the history of the artists and the subject matter of the painting.

"This is most interesting. It says that her dress represents pomegranates, a symbol of righteousness and fruitfulness. She died of malaria in 1562 along with her son Giovanni pictured with her in this painting by Bronzino."

"Interesting but...."

"Wait! There's more.

It says that she used the pomegranate symbol frequently because it was reintroduced into Italy by her father's (Don Pedro of Toledo) chief of staff, Don Gaetano Catalano, Marquis of Gonzales."

"What?

Are you kidding me?"

"Look. It's right here in black and white."

His eyes transfixed on the plaque, validating that what she said was real.

"Well, I'll be."

He read it aloud several times.

"And it says that Don Gaetano relocated to Catanzaro after Don Pedro was transferred to Siena in 1552."

He turned back to her.

"Catanzaro?

Do you know where that is?"

"I'm not sure. I think it's in southern Italy somewhere...perhaps Calabria. But I'd have to look it up on a map."

"Then why don't we head back to the hotel and see if we can locate it on the map. I think Catanzaro should be our next stop."

*

The couple returned to Campagna with the intent of making Catanzaro the next destination on their quest for Don Gaetano Catalano. While they knew that by some whim of fate his ancestors eventually settled in Maria's home town, the unknowns were why and when.

But suddenly it occurred to him that they might have to postpone that visit. He had originally planned a two week excursion to Italy and by the time of their return to Campagna from Tuscany, he realized that his return date to Georgia was at hand.

"Maria, I know that this is somewhat sudden, but why don't you come back to Atlanta with me...and perhaps consider making the arrangement permanent?"

She gasped.

"Does this mean you want to marry me?"

He was reticent to propose formally just yet.

"I think it could very well work out that way."

She carefully weighed his words, not being exactly pleased by his answer.

"You know, I still don't know precisely what it is you do in Atlanta. You've been a bit vague."

"I told you that I'm in the import/export business. What exactly I deal in varies from time to time depending on opportunity and need."

She found his answer still vague...perhaps even more so than the first time she posed the question at their first meeting.

"As tempting as your offer sounds, I need to finish disposing of my mother's things and decide on what to do with her estate.

And besides, I don't have a passport. Here in my country it can take some time to secure one.

Anyway, I can be your contact here should you need something researched."

"I take it that's a polite way of saying 'no'?"

"Not 'no'...just not right now.

Why don't I plan on coming to America when I get my things settled here? Then we can see if our feelings are the same...and I am sure they will be...at least for me."

"I think I can safely say they will be for me as well."

They moved closer to one another and stood in a quiet embrace.

Maria suddenly wondered silently if giving herself to him had all been a huge mistake.

"Then it's settled. As soon as I get home I'll start making plans for you to come to Georgia. There are so many things I'd like to show you. But first I'll need to come back here to continue my family quest."

She hoped his words confirmed that she had not been wrong in her judgment of him and his feelings for her.

PART TWO

CHAPTER TEN

"Maria!
Hi.
Good news.

I've arranged my affairs here at home so that I can come back to Italy in about three weeks. How will that work with your schedule?"

She was taken aback by the suddenness of his message. He had been gone for almost a week, and except for calling to say that he had arrived safely, there had been total silence. She had begun to have doubts about his intentions.

"I'm getting things done with my mother's affairs and should be mostly under control within the month. And I've applied for a passport so we can also make plans for my visit to Georgia.

So that should work well."

"Besides, I've missed you", he said softly.

She let his words settle gently into her ears...and her heart.

"And I've missed you, too."

Maria had hoped that the word "love" would be among his words of greeting. But she decided to settle for the knowledge that he would be returning.

"You know I've had a chance to research Catanzaro. It is in Calabria as I suspected...on the east side of southern Italy overlooking the Ionian Sea. There is a lido portion of the town less than three miles away. It should be beautiful at this time of year."

"Lido...that's some kind of beach isn't it?

Perhaps if you have time you could find us a nice place to stay there while we do some research on Don Gaetano. And perhaps we can find some time to enjoy the water...when we're not enjoying each other."

"That sounds perfect" she conveyed with an intimacy in her voice.

Though she couldn't see his face, she knew that he was smiling on the other end of the phone.

"I can't wait.

We'll work out the details when I get back to Italy."

*

This time he flew through Paris's Charles de Gaulle airport. After a brief layover, his Air France flight brought him directly into Naples where Maria eagerly awaited his arrival.

When she saw him appear on the escalator heading toward the baggage claim area, she waved from outside the security fence to let him know that she was there as promised.

Another thirty minutes elapsed before he finally exited from passport control and walked hurriedly in her direction.

"Oh I've missed you so" she said as he embraced her.

"And I've missed you too" he responded with a passionate kiss firmly on her lips.

"So, what's the plan?"

She looked at him somewhat quizzically.

He understood the look and realized she didn't comprehend his colloquialism.

"I mean, what have you arranged for us in Catanzaro?"

"Oh" she said with a grin.

"You must forgive me for not understanding some of your sayings."

"I forgive you" he replied as he took her hand and she led them to the exit for the parking garage.

"I thought we would spend tonight at my place since it's on the way to Catanzaro. Then we can leave in the morning...its only about three hundred and fifty kilometers...about two hundred miles."

He smiled.

"They tried to change us Americans to the metric system many years ago, but it just didn't work. But that's all right...I know how to convert the two."

He placed his suitcase and several small bags in the trunk of her Fiat...they barely fit...and then jumped into the passenger seat.

"See how fast you can get us to Campagna. I've got a lot to tell you since we last talked...and a few things I'd like to show you up close and personal!"

*

"What did you want to tell me?" Maria asked as they entered her front door and moved into the living room.

"Actually, it wasn't so much what I wanted to tell you as what I wanted to show you...or both."

He reached into his tote bag and pulled out a small box, the kind usually found in a jewelry store.

He dropped down onto one knee, and opened the box exposing a large solitaire diamond.

"Maria Rosato" he started.

"I've spent a miserable month at home without you. All I could do during my waking hours was think about you and our time together here in Italy. And well...

Will you marry me?"

Though his words didn't come as a total surprise, she gasped just the same.

"O yes! O yes!" she replied with the enthusiasm and glee of a school girl.

"Jack, of course I'll marry you.

I was so afraid that I had put you off with my aloofness before you left for home.

I've been just as miserable the whole time you were gone. Everyday while I was working around the house readying things to give away, I thought only of you and our times together...and wondered...hoped...that you would come back and want me as much as I want you."

She extended her left hand and watched as he slid the ring onto her fourth finger.

"It fits perfectly...how did you know my size?

And it's so big.

Two carats?"

"Two and a half. And I occasionally handle jewelry in my business, so I'm pretty good at estimating ring sizes.

It looks beautiful on you!"

She squealed again as she held her hand out in front of her and eyed it from every angle.

"I wish mother could be here at this moment."

She paused to reflect on the past.

Then after a few moments of silence, the couple hurried to her bedroom where they consummated their engagement promises.

Their time apart was at an end.

*

The following day they drove the short distance from Campagna through Eboli; then turning east and south onto the A3, the route took them all the way into Calabria. Their early start had been interrupted by a prolonged love making session so that it was late morning when they made the entrance onto the autostrada.

The sun reflected brightly on the windshield. The air was refreshingly cool thanks to a light breeze from the east.

"I hope you brought sun glasses?" she asked as she donned her fashionable Oakley shades.

He reached into his jacket pocket and held up his Ray Ban aviators; after waving them under her nose, he put them on.

"I didn't want you to think you're the only one with any fashion sense" he mused.

She gave him a slightly contemptuous look and then continued.

"We'll be getting into the mountains in a little while" she advised him.

"I know a quaint place in Mormanno where we can have a late lunch. It's called the Chalet Rocco and it's just off the A3. Their food is wonderful and the scenery breathtaking. It's situated in the Pollino National Park at about eleven hundred meters…that would be thirty-five hundred feet…above sea level."

"You continue to amaze me with your knowledge of various parts of Italy. It sounds perfect.

But I thought you said you hadn't been here before?"

"I told you my late husband dealt in antique manuscripts. Seeking them out took us to almost every part of Italy at one time or another.

I've never been to Catanzaro, but I have been all the way to the tip of the 'boot' of Italy on the A3. That's where you can take the ferry to Messina on Sicily. We toured the island following a meeting with a dealer in Palermo.

You should let me take you there some time. It's very romantic."

Almost an hour later, after negotiating a number of changes in elevation and passing several promontories with beautiful vistas, they arrived at the Campotenese exit from the A3. Moments later they approached Chalet Rocco.

Their window table afforded them a panoramic view of the magnificent countryside.

While quietly enjoying each others company and gazing at the beautiful scenery, she suddenly blurted out something that had been nagging at her since his arrival.

"You didn't say what else you did while you were at home... other than miss me that is."

Holding her hand across the table, he squeezed it at the sound of her voice.

"Well, aside from taking care of some business, I did have time to do a little research about Don Gaetano and Catanzaro and Campagna. But the facts are very sketchy on the internet.

I also contacted several relatives of mine in New York and Connecticut...that's where my grandparents lived. These were people that I really don't know but had their names given me years ago by some of my relatives who lived there but are no longer living.

Most of the conversations with the ones that I was able to reach were somewhat strained. You know it's funny that most people don't seem to care much about where their ancestors came from, what they did or even what nationality they were.

Several of them were reluctant to talk at all...almost like they didn't believe I was who I said I was. It's funny...I've thought about it quite a bit...and I still can't figure out what someone thinks you might be after when you've given them your name and the connection to their family...and all you want in return is some additional facts about the family genealogy. I guess most people think there has to be an ulterior motive...that you're hoping they'll reveal some fact about a family member that would make them a target for a robbery or worse."

"It's different for me" said Maria.

"Here we are all Italian and our relatives usually came from the same town or at least the same region of the country. Of course we do have some immigrants from surrounding areas in the Mediterranean, but they make up a minority. And...most Italians love to talk...especially about their families."

"I had one particularly interesting...if not downright weird... conversation with someone I thought was a relative. I had the phone number of a Salvatore Catalano in New York City, a person I was led to believe was related to me distantly.

When I called the number, a woman named Rosa answered the phone. I explained to her who I was and why I was calling. She kept asking me if I was trying to reach 'Toto'. I didn't have any idea what she meant by that so after a while I thanked her and hung up.

Well, the following day I got a call from someone calling himself Joe Ganci asking why I was trying to reach Sal Catalano. He didn't seem to accept the fact that I was just doing genealogy research. The following day I got another call from a friend of his...someone named Licati.

I don't mind telling you the whole thing was a bit unnerving. I looked Salvatore Catalano up on the internet and found that his nickname is 'Toto' and that he became a mafia don in this country after the murder of one of the big bosses named Carmine Galante, and that he was sent to prison some years ago for his involvement in a drug trafficking scheme called the 'pizza connection' since they were importing drugs from Sicily to New York through stores that fronted as pizzerias."

She looked at him with genuine concern in her eyes.

"Perhaps you just called the wrong person of the same name. There are many people with those particular names here in Italy. I would imagine with the large number of Italians in New York that the same would hold true there too."

"You're probably right.

Well, let's enjoy our lunch."

"Would you excuse me for a moment? I need to 'powder my nose'...at least, I think that's how you would say it in America."

"Very good! You're learning. But don't be too long." He smiled as she disappeared around the corner.

After secluding herself in one of the bathroom stalls, she reached into her purse for her phone and placed a call.

*

They sat and talked while the waiter cleared the table.

"You know, you haven't mentioned yet where and when you'd like to get married."

Maria looked at him with a contentment she had not shared with anyone for a long time.

"Since mother is gone, I feel that we can plan that at our leisure. I don't want another big church wedding...I've already had that. Without any family, it's not that important any more.

Being with you is all that I care about.

What about you, though?

Does any of your family know about me?

And would you like a big wedding?"

He reflected on her questions momentarily before answering. "No. Not really.

A big wedding ceremony is just not that important to most men, I guess. My parents are dead and I don't have any siblings. Except for the distant relatives I mentioned earlier, all the immediate aunts and uncles on my mother's side of the family are gone. I only have one cousin from mother's four siblings, and he's not married. He lives somewhere in Massachusetts.

I have a lot of cousins and second cousins on my father's side who mostly live in Georgia, but I never see or hear from any of them.

The most important thing to me is our being together.

So why don't we give it a little thought and then make plans accordingly?"

"I'd like that."

They shared a piece of Tiramisu for dessert along with espresso.

"Well, I guess if we're going to get to Catanzaro before dark, we'd better get going."

"Yes, we'd better.

I wish we had time to drive just west of here. I know you'd love the view of the Tyrrhenian Sea from the lookout point. It's so beautiful."

"Why not make time?

Right now, I feel like we have all the time in the world."

The road towards Avena was serpentine and extremely narrow all the way. They chose to stop at the overlook where the view of the rocky coast and Tyrrhenian Sea was breathtaking. From there to the coastline would have been all down hill...and extremely time consuming. So, after a brief interlude, they decided it time to retrace their steps to the A3 and turn south towards Calabria.

"Maria, these months with you have been the best in my life. The way I feel today...well, I just don't know what I would have done if you hadn't volunteered to help me with my ancestor search that day I came into the museum.

Otherwise...well who knows what the rest of our lives would have been like?"

With her head now resting on his shoulder, she just purred like a kitten who had just tasted her mother's milk for the first time.

They each felt a genuine contentment in their lives that neither had experienced in a long while.

*

The remainder of the journey to Catanzaro brought them through a series of mountain passes, over high vistas, and along lush valleys interspersed with towns previously unknown to him and generally to Maria as well. He was amazed that many of them had populations of forty or fifty thousand or more, and took at least ten minutes to traverse due to antiquated stop light systems and occasional one lane sections of road that only allowed traffic to pass in one direction at a time.

Despite having studied maps of the roads of Italy and even viewed Italy on Google Earth, the terrain continued to amaze him, much as it had when he first set eyes on the Apennines on his first visit to Campagna. The road soared to altitudes above three or four thousand feet and then plunged back into valleys only a few hundred feet above sea level.

The tunnels particularly fascinated him. Europe is known for its long tunnels, especially in Austria and Switzerland, and Italy proved to be no exception. Had they not been constructed through the high peaks of the Parco Pollino, he wasn't sure just how long it might have taken to reach their destination.

Around five o'clock, they finally arrived at Catanzaro and were pleasantly surprised by its quaintness and tranquility. The view of the Ionian Sea in the distance was at least as spectacular as the views of the Tyrrhenian Sea they had experienced earlier in the day.

Maria had made arrangements for their stay near the town center.

From the piazza Matteotti, the Il Cedro bed and breakfast was only a short distance south and they found it easily, registered and settled into the room before dark.

It was a far cry from the lavishness of their near Florentine hotel. But it was comfortable, the staff was friendly and the rooms well appointed. They dined at a nearby restaurant and then retired to their room.

Finding Don Gaetano Catalano would be their main agenda for the following day.

CHAPTER ELEVEN

The seventeenth century was in its infancy as Francesco Catalano made his way to the Campania region of Italy. The small town of Campagna in the hills just north of Eboli held promise for him, being in need of someone with legal and banking skills. He felt confident that he had studied banking with the best mentors of the day... the Medici in Florence. His legal skills he considered adequate at best.

Campagna's location, nestled in the crevice of two converging mountain ridges, lent itself well to protection from anyone who might wish the town harm. A small armed band of men had been hired by the town officials to provide added protection in any event. Their leader was Don Bartolo Cenci, a name known only to his closest associates. To the people of the Campania region he bore the title *"Il Garrotta"* – "the strangler" after his preferred method of execution for those that tried to move against the town or him or his band of men.

Despite being in the city's employ, Don Bartolo had made perfectly clear to the merchants of Campagna his need for a little extra reward for the bands protection and had instituted a policy of monthly tribute collections from each of them.

Francesco had easily ensconced himself into the small town and by sixteen hundred and two had opened a bank patterned after the system taught him by the Medici. In addition, he had offered his services in legal matters to the town council.

*

"Don Catalano, may I presume that you know who I am?"

The imposing figure of a man stood in the entrance to the bank at a moment when no customers were present.

Francesco glanced toward the source of the voice.

"And what can I do for my friend Don Bartolo today?

Perhaps you would like me to arrange a loan, Il Garrotta?"

"So you do know who I am?

Then you must also know why I am here?"

"I have heard rumors. But you must know that the city relies on me to keep its finances intact and to advise it on legal matters. Without me and my bank, many people who you expect to compensate you for your 'protection' would not always have the funds to do so…including the city itself."

Don Bartolo stood silent for a few moments, absorbing Francesco's words.

"Don Francesco, you are a brave man to say that to my face… and what you say may well be true.

Perhaps then we can make a deal, for I am a reasonable man.

You protect the assets of all those who owe me money, and I will protect you without need for any 'tribute.'"

Francesco knew better than to challenge the man. After pretending to give his offer consideration for a brief moment, he answered.

"Then we have a deal.

And it will remain our secret."

"Yes" said Don Bartolo.

It shall be ours alone."

Don Bartolo stepped forward into the bank, tipped his hat toward Francesco and then quickly and quietly disappeared.

*

The following morning they were up early, ready to begin their quest for Don Gaetano.

They drove to the city hall.

"Now, all we have to do is find a place to park."

Parking can be somewhat confusing in many Italian cities since there is generally some type of metered ticket dispenser often located remotely from street parking places. The ticket once obtained is usually then displayed on the dashboard of the car where it can be seen by police patrols.

With Maria's help and knowledge of local customs they quickly secured a place, obtained a ticket and placed it on the dash.

"Thank God you're with me. This parking business in foreign countries leaves me totally confused. I always have this fear of coming back and finding my car gone...and then trying to figure out where to go and how to retrieve it...hopefully without costing me a fortune.

Now, let's see if we can find any information about my relatives."

*

They began their quest by locating the town records depository. The receptionist at the information desk at city hall directed them to the library contained within the same structure that housed an antiquary section with records dating back several hundred years or more.

Fortunately, Maria's ability to converse in the native language afforded them one less barrier to cross.

"I hope the records are fully indexed and accessible by computer. Some of these cities still look and act like they are living in a previous century. From the looks of Catanzaro, I'm going to bet that it's not one of them."

When they arrived at the room housing the old documents, they found that they could access them from a computer index, view the documents on line and in many cases see the originals.

They sat at separate computer terminals and began searching.

After only a short time, Maria almost shouted.

"Here's a reference to a Gaetano Catalano."

He stood and looked over her shoulder at the computer screen.

"I'm afraid that can't be the right one.

It says he lived in the eighteen hundreds."

"Oh." She let out a deflated sigh.

"Sorry" she uttered in a low tone.

"That's all right, my love. Keep trying."

She turned and reached for his hand and smiled fondly at him.

"That's the first time you called me 'my love'" she said in a whisper.

"It won't be the last."

Jack bent down and lightly kissed her.

She looked around to make sure no one was watching them.

"Save that for later." She smiled demurely.

"That must have been what DaVinci saw in his subject for the Mona Lisa" he retorted, referring to her smile.

"Let's get back to work."

*

Half the morning disappeared before either of them uttered another remark.

"I think I have something here" he finally declared.

Maria stood over his shoulder staring at the computer screen.

"It says that there was a Don Gaetano Catalano here in the fifteen hundreds and that he was a prominent merchant. This town was the center of the cloth trade, especially silk and velvet. I remember reading something about that earlier."

He scrolled down the article.

"Look, there's a link here to some other information about him."

He clicked on the link and impatiently waited for the new article to appear.

"The History of the Cloth Trade in Catanzaro Italy in the Sixteenth and Seventeenth Centuries."

Their excitement built as they considered the possibilities that this article might hold. They scrolled quickly looking for a reference to Don Gaetano. After only a few minutes and almost twenty pages of the manuscript, he shouted:

"Look.

It says that Don Gaetano Catalano was a prominent merchant here in the mid- and latter fifteen hundreds, and that he came from Naples where he was associated with Don Pedro of Toledo.

It's him...it has to be" he exploded with enthusiasm.

Maria smiled and caressed his shoulders.

"I think you've found your long lost relative.

Read on!"

*

Reading articles on the Internet on a computer wasn't exactly like reading the Sunday morning paper or looking at pictures in an issue of National Geographic.

There were often portions written in English and portions written in Italian and occasionally interspersed with other languages. Illustrations were often captioned in foreign languages or written using a Gothic style font that made it even more difficult to decipher.

By early afternoon he decided it was time for a long overdue break.

"What do you say we break for lunch?

I'm not used to sitting on hard chairs for this length of time."

"I think we're finally making some headway" Maria replied as they exited the record room where they had been ensconced for almost four hours.

"I think I noticed a small *trattoria* near where we parked the car. Perhaps a little pasta and wine will perk us up for a later session with those files" she added.

"Lead on" he responded

They located La Cava without difficulty. The food typically was homemade and delicious. The wine...a red Nero d'Avola from nearby Sicily...complemented the pasta sampler they ordered that afforded them a taste of five different regional dishes.

"I still don't know how you Italians can eat all this starchy food and remain so slim", he noted once again. He was already feeling full and slowly ate as he watched her continue to devour items from each plate.

"Even though I'm pretty full and know we have a lot more work to do today, I can't resist trying their cannoli. How about you?"

"I'm a Tiramisu lover" he responded. I just have to sample it everywhere I go. It's rare to find a bad recipe anywhere in my country."

"Then let's get one of each and share."

They ate slowly exchanging forkfuls.

"Which do you like best?" Maria asked.

"You" was his answer.

She smiled.

"Thank you.

Now, let's finish our coffee and get back to work. I want to see just where you came from and who it was that made you so sweet."

*

"The remainder of the afternoon melted away as they continued to read the long and tedious document that had tweaked their curiosity with the mention of Don Gaetano early on but then seemed to turn to matters totally unrelated.

They were on the verge of calling it a day when Maria once more squealed.

"I think I've got something.

Look", she said pointing to the paragraph at the bottom of the current page. It was in Italian.

"Roughly translated, it says that Don Gaetano married the daughter of another prominent merchant, a Don Juan de Salas in the year fifteen hundred and fifty-five. Her name was Margherite. Together they had seven children. It doesn't mention any of them except for Antonio, the second child and by Italian custom one not entitled to any inheritance. He apparently left Catanzaro sometime after the death of his father in fifteen hundred and seventy and settled in Monteleone.

That's all there is."

She turned and looked at him.

"Where is Monteleone?" he asked.

"I'm not sure. We'll need to look it up on one of the search engines."

They found the Italian equivalent of **Google** and entered the name. They were surprised...and pleased...when they saw that the town had changed its name to Vibo Valentia and that it too was in Calabria...and only about fifty miles from where they were.

"Well, I guess we can do a little more research here, but then I think our next stop has to be Vibo"...as they decided to label it for simplicity sake.

"It fits the description in your great uncle's letter that you descend from a non-inheriting son of Don Gaetano" she remarked.

"I wonder why there is no mention of the inheriting son... whatever his name was?"

"I'm sure I don't know, but you amaze me that you remember every little detail of things that are not even part of your family or history."

"Not yet" Maria replied.

"But soon?" she queried.

"Soon" he replied.

Jack took her hand and led her to the car. Once in their room, they spoke of wedding plans as they explored each other's bodies.

They would leave for Vibo in the morning.

*

Times were bad and getting worse in seventeenth century Campagna. Don Francesco Catalano's bank was on the verge of failure along with most enterprises in the small town.

He was somewhat apprehensive at the sudden appearance of Don Bartolo Cenci in his doorway.

"Don Bartolo, you humble me with your presence.

What may I help you with today?"

Il Garrotto's demeanor was ominous. He stood with his right arm folded behind him as if hiding something.

"Don Francesco, some time ago we made a deal that you would protect my business interests, and I and my men in turn would protect you at no cost to you personally.

But you have let me down. My collections continue to dwindle and I cannot afford to let that happen."

Don Francesco stood his ground, clutching an object in his right hand while maintaining his distance from his adversary.

"Don Bartolo, you know that times are difficult for everyone right now. I have done all that I can within my power to assure that those you protect, those who pay you money for that service, are as financially secure as I can make them."

Don Francesco disliked the imposing look Don Bartolo projected, as well as the tone of his voice as he spoke.

He began to move toward Don Francesco.

"I will not be made a fool of by anyone in this town, especially not a lowly banker who I hear has taken to hiding the money of those who rightfully owe it to me...."

"I know of no such thing.

Who would tell you such an untruth?"

"That is of little consequence to you now, Don Francesco."

Don Bartolo was already at the feet of Don Francesco and reaching for his neck with the garrote that he now displayed in his right hand.

"Take this, banker thief!"

Without a word of response, Don Francesco silently drew the knife he held in his right hand and plunged it into Don Bartolo's chest, piercing his heart and killing him instantly.

Blood splattered in every direction as Don Bartolo's body fell to the floor. Don Francesco stared down at his crimson colored tunic.

He remained motionless and silent as he contemplated the act he had just committed.

"My God! I have killed a man.

And not just any man...but Don Bartolo, a thief among thieves, and head of the most notorious gang in all of Campania.

I must get away fast. But first I must dispose of the body, before someone finds it here and assumes correctly that I am the one who committed this foul act."

He locked the establishment door and turned to the work at hand. He found a length of cloth and wrapped the body in it. He cleaned all stains of blood that had dripped onto the floor and walls. He then changed into a fresh tunic and placed the soiled one into the cloth covering Don Bartolo's body. Then waiting until dark, he took the corpse and dumped it into the small river that ran through town, counting on the current to wash it down stream far away from Campagna.

As he returned to the bank, he pondered the situation further and concluded that running would be the wrong move...that it would make him highly suspect of the murder if Don Bartolo's body was ultimately found.

Don Francesco reinspected his property, assuring himself that all traces of the misdeed were erased and that everything had been restored to its proper place and appearance.

He would be open for business as usual the following day.

Chapter Twelve

Early the following morning, after a leisurely breakfast in the European tradition with fruits and cheeses, cold meats, muesli cereal and coffee, the couple made their way towards Vibo Valentia. They retraced their steps, a short fifteen miles from Catanzaro to the junction with the A3, and then turned south.

The road paralleled the Tyrrhenian Sea for a short while and then advanced up a steep hill to the outer edges of the town.

"There's a welcome center a mile ahead" Maria remarked, as they passed a sign written in Italian that announced its location.

He slowed down in advance of stopping, pulled into the parking lot indicated by a small sign and then escorted her into the diminutive building.

There were numerous pamphlets describing the history of the town and the region, local and regional points of interest, and business directories promoting local eating and sleeping establishments.

"It says here that the name of the town was changed from Monteleone to its original Roman name, Vibo Valentia, in nineteen hundred and twenty-eight. It was originally colonized by the Greeks and called Hipponion. The first settlers were from Locri around seven hundred B.C. It was also under the control of Syracusa...that's Sicily; and by several Italian tribes and then Carthage. After the Carthaginians were defeated by Rome in the second Punic war, around one ninety-two B.C. it remained mostly under control of Italy who renamed it Vibo Valentia. However, it was briefly controlled by the Spanish Aragonese, and in the ninth century by the Saracen raiders and then the Normans, who built a castle on the site of the original Greek acropolis above the town.

It was during the reign of Emperor Frederick II in the thirteenth century, then the Holy Roman Emperor and King of Sicily, that he renamed it Monteleone…Mount of the Lion. The town ultimately became a part of the Kingdom of the Two Sicilies and subsequently the Italian nation after the unification that occurred during the eighteen sixties. It was the fascist regime that controlled Italy until the fall of Mussolini towards the end of World War II that returned it to its original Roman name."

"Well! That was a mouth full. I think I now know more than I needed to know about the naming business."

Maria cast him a slightly annoyed look…after all, it was an important part of what they had come to learn.

"I'm sorry. You're right. I was very brusque with you and I apologize."

Maria smiled and acknowledged his apology.

"Now, what do you say we do a little sightseeing and have lunch before we get down to the business of looking for Antonio Catalano?" he added.

*

The members of Don Bartolo's gang wasted no time in confronting Don Francesco. They knew of the rivalry that had existed between the two and immediately suspected that he might be involved with their leader's mysterious disappearance. During Don Bartolo's last contact with them, he had indicated that he planned to meet the banker.

As he watched their stealthy approach, Don Francesco knew he must seize the moment. He boldly announced to the assemblage that he had killed their leader and was now assuming leadership of the group. Since none of them had ever been more than a follower, they promptly acquiesced.

"Now, I will tell you what we must do to regain our status in the town and the region" he enthusiastically proclaimed to them.

Who among you doesn't want to have money and power again?"

Similar to a lightning strike, a miraculous transformation occurred. In the space of a moment, Don Francesco Catalano the banker became a confessed murderer assuming control of a leaderless and lawless band of thugs.

"*Il Coltello*" one of the gang members addressed him as he marched forward to bow and kiss his hand.

The others followed in similar fashion.

He recognized that they knew the manner of death he had perpetrated on his predecessor.

"Yes! From now on I will be called 'Il Coltello' – the knife."

*

The years that followed the creation and rise of "Il Coltello" were replete with tales of his gang ravishing the countryside of Campania. Reports of travelers being ambushed, homes and businesses being robbed and various protection schemes being proffered continued to surface. Local authorities remained helpless to control the marauding band that had grown in size to as many as fifty or more according to various reports.

Throughout the period that his band remained actively in control of the Campania region, Don Francesco maintained his façade as a proper money lender in the small village of Campagna and maintained his domicile in a villa he had constructed on the edge of town.

Although he had given little thought to marriage during the active years of his gang, he was fast becoming aware of his advancing age and the need for an heir to whom he could entrust his holdings.

Early in the year sixteen hundred and fourteen, he was introduced to Lucretia Campanezzi by her father, Don Marco Campanezzi, a leading merchant in Campagna as well as a business associate and client of Don Francesco.

Lucretia was almost ten years younger than Francesco. Her father, however, eager to secure a good husband for her, approached Don Francesco with an offer that he found impossible to refuse. In addition to his voluptuous young daughter, Don Marco pledged eternal loyalty and full financial partnership in all his business concerns.

"Don Marco, I will accept your offer, for your daughter is beautiful and your terms are more than generous.

How could a man refuse?"

He presented his future father-in-law a goblet of wine and proposed a toast.

Don Marco thanked him profusely, again pledging his loyalty.

"Of course, I will remain in your protection as before" he said, making reference to the agreement that Don Francesco had inherited when he seized leadership of the late Don Bartolo's gang.

"Yes! It is a good arrangement.

Let us drink to that as well."

*

The glorious ceremony was celebrated late morning on a warm spring day, the fifth of June, sixteen hundred and fourteen at the Basilica di Santa Maria della Pace, the seat of Catholicism in Campagna and presided over by the current archbishop, Gaetano Pollio.

The entire village was in attendance since no one would dare to offend the bridegroom, *Il Coltello*. In an effort to be known more politely in public, since a portion of the community was not familiar with the more nefarious portions of his business, he demanded that he be addressed as *Il Padrino*...or simply ***Godfather.***

As soon as the formal ceremony had concluded, he excused himself as his bride was readying herself for the reception.

"My dear Lucretia, I have a little business to conduct while your bridesmaids attend you. Please excuse me." He leaned in and kissed her lightly on the cheek.

Moving to a room adjacent to the reception area, he gathered together several of his gang members and instructed them to collect the tributes being left by the many patrons at the festive event.

"And do not be afraid to let them know that they are welcome to add to the gifts that they have already delivered!"

"We will see to it, *Il Padrino*."

*

The festivities had continued on well into the evening.

Lucretia's day had been long and exhausting. It had begun with early mass and sacraments, followed by breakfast with the women of the family and the wedding party. Getting dressed had occupied almost two hours before she was ushered by waiting coach to the church. And now another ten hours had elapsed since the new couple had exited the church en route to the post-nuptial festivities.

She shamelessly wished that she and her new husband might retire to their bed as she was anxious to find out if what she had heard about men on their wedding night was true. The women of the family...her mother most prominently...had warned her that sexual relations between a man and a woman was her "duty" and not necessarily to be enjoyed.

Two of her older married sisters had intimated that while it was a duty and sometimes painful, it was also something that secretly gave them great pleasure.

Lucretia eagerly anticipated her own personal experience.

Approaching midnight, Francesco came for her and the couple bid goodnight to the assemblage. Retired to their bedchamber, she stood before him and slowly lowered the shoulder straps from her wedding dress gradually exposing her perfect breasts. He kissed her neck as her dress fell to the floor leaving her totally naked.

As he caressed her now fully erect nipples, his hand proceeded slowly down her side onto her buttocks and then around to the cleft in her pubic area. Her bosom heaved as the newfound pleasure wrapped her in all consuming delight. She could feel the moisture gathering between her legs in full anticipation of his entrance.

Turning to find the bed on which to lie, Lucretia was suddenly jolted from her rapture when Francesco suddenly and inexplicably slapped her across the face, sending her reeling to the floor.

Stunned by his unprovoked and wholly unanticipated violent action, she recoiled to the corner dazed, and utterly confused by this sudden personality transformation.

"You are now my wife and from this day on you will do what I say.

You will care for my house, make my meals and attend my sexual needs. You will have my children and you will raise them properly.

You will not discuss these personal matters with anyone unless I so approve.

In return for your loyalty, I will treat you properly and respectfully. No one will have cause to think otherwise of our commitment to one another.

But...if you try to convince anyone that I am not the person that I profess to be...I will devise a way to have you killed!"

Lucretia sobbed bitterly as she lay helplessly alone and naked on the floor, not knowing what to do or what to say or how to react on the most anticipated day of her life that had just been transformed into her worst nightmare.

Expecting...and getting no response from his wife...Francesco slowly helped her up from the floor, laid her on the bed and without hesitation proceeded to consummate their marriage. As she whimpered, he withdrew from her, dressed and then turned toward her.

"Now, I will sleep in another room. If it pleases me to do so, I will find you in the morning" he uttered as he slammed the bedroom door.

Ashamed and abandoned, she quietly sobbed herself to sleep, wondering what she had done to deserve such a fate.

CHAPTER THIRTEEN

The first stop on their sightseeing tour of Vibo was a climb to the top of the belvedere grande where a spectacular view stretched from the Sila Mountains in the Calabrian central province westward to the mighty peak of Mt. Aetna on the island of Sicily.

Nearby were ruins that included a Norman castle, built centuries later on the same site as the earlier Roman remnants that included several preserved houses and thermal baths. Old walls and the skeleton of a Doric temple told of ancient Greek occupation that preceded the Romans.

No Italian city would be complete without its complement of churches, and Vibo Valentia was no exception. Prominent were the Duomo, built in Baroque style and the Chiesa Sant Michele constructed in Renaissance mode, each dating to fifteen hundred and nineteen.

After brief stops at several museums that housed artifacts from both the Roman and Greek occupations of the area, the couple concluded their sightseeing and made their way to the government center where they presumed the historical library would be located.

Fortunately, their assumption was correct.

Allied bombing during World War II had inflicted severe damage on many cities and towns in the vicinity of Vibo. Municipal buildings had been a primary target of the attacks. Fortunately, Vibo's had been spared.

The municipal centers library held a vast collection of volumes. A quick scan of the data preserved, now maintained on computer files, led them to information dating from the late sixteenth century.

"I continue to be amazed at all the original books and documents still in existence, especially here in Europe, where there have been so many wars over the centuries.

But then the more I think about it, I guess it's true in every country. Thank God for people with foresight who took the time to preserve these important vestiges of the past for future generations.

Maria, did I ever tell you about the time I was looking for some of my father's relatives in Petersburg, Virginia? While I was looking through some old record books, mostly of tax papers and the like, I found a document signed by Thomas Jefferson himself.

And then there was the time in Philadelphia that the record librarian told me that a volume I wanted had been 'checked out' in a part of the library that shouldn't have allowed it. When I pressed her on it, she said I could go across the street and see the original... and I did.

It was a letter handwritten by one of my ancestors in the seventeen hundred and sixties.

But I'm digressing."

"That's all right" said Maria. "I like it when you tell me very personal things about your life. This Thomas Jefferson...he was one of your presidents, yes?"

"Yes!

Very good. You know American history." He smiled and patted her hand.

Turning back to their computer search, it wasn't long until he got a "hit" on Antonio Catalano.

"According to this, he was the ***capo guardacaccia*** here for many years but that he left and went to Florence to live with his son, Francesco, after the death of his wife. That was in the late fifteen hundreds. Francesco went to apprentice with Ferdinando di Medici."

"Are you sure it's the right one?" she asked.

"It says he came from Catanzaro. It would be quite a coincidence if there had been more than one I would think...it's the right name and right time period.

We can look a little more, but I think we're on to something. And again, there's mention of the Medicis and Florence.

It seems as if we are going in that proverbial circle."

Since the day was late, he proposed returning the following morning. If they couldn't find any information to suggest a more direct connection to Campagna, then they would make their way back to Florence.

*

After an exhaustive but fruitless second effort the following day, they concluded that what they had found earlier had to be correct. Accordingly, they exited the town en route back to Tuscany.

The journey back to Firenze was most enjoyable in anticipation of what they were hoping to discover concerning the Catalano family when they reached there.

Since the route to Florence passed close to Campagna, they decided to spend the night at Maria's. As they approached the Eboli exit at the supper hour, a thought suddenly flashed through Jack's mind.

"Let's have dinner at Pasquales. It is sort of 'our place'...where we shared our first meal together.

It seems like yesterday, although you know it's already been more than a month."

"I'm so comfortable being with you, that only time away from you makes me aware of the clock ticking anymore.

Let's do stop there for dinner" Maria replied enthusiastically.

They shared plans for their future together over a meal of homemade pasta and wine before returning to her home. Getting to Florence and continuing the search for Antonio and Francesco Catalano remained their goal for the following day.

*

The following morning, Saturday, got off to a slower start than originally planned. Maria had insisted on preparing a breakfast, following which the couple lingered in bed, enjoying one last round of love making.

"It's the weekend anyway" she opined.

"We'll motor slowly to Bagno and stay at Villa il Calle as before. I'll call and make sure they have my suite available.

Since tomorrow is Sunday, perhaps we can just do a little sightseeing in Florence and save the research for Monday morning. There are so many things to see and do there and we've only scratched the surface...I think that's how you say it in America?"

"It's perfect...your English and one of our funny little sayings."

"I'd like to show you as many of Firenze's attractions as you'd like to see."

"With you, I would walk the streets of Florence until the soles of my shoes have holes in them."

She looked at him in that strange and bewildered way.

Then she laughed.

"That's another of your funny little sayings, I'm guessing?"

"Yep.

Now, why don't we shower together and then get going?"

*

The shower slowed them down once again. The sensuousness of it lulled them back into bed once more...but finally they were dressed and in the Fiat moving toward Eboli en route to Florence. The day was clear and Vesuvius loomed large in the distance as they passed northwest towards Naples.

"Can you imagine what would happen if that thing were to erupt again? It's been several thousand years since the last major eruption and according to some experts it's about time for it to blow again."

She sat in relative silence for a few moments.

"I've read the reports on those theories, and I don't mind telling you that it really frightens me. Virtually all of Naples and most of the surrounding countryside for fifty or a hundred miles could be wiped out, depending on how long the eruption lasted and in which direction it blew most of its toxic products.

It's one reason that I'm glad I no longer have to decide on returning to live in Naples or Campania.

You know, you've said very little about where you think we ought to live after we're married...or for that matter when the big date should be."

"Well, my love, we said the other day that we thought it ought to be soon, so what do you say?...you decide.

Why not head to America as soon as we finish our search for my ancestors and tie the knot?"

"Tie the knot?" Maria retorted.

They both laughed.

"I know...another of your cute American expressions."

"Yes!

It means to get married". Jack explained.

"And after our honeymoon...and I think I know just the place for that...we can return to Atlanta and decide if we want to stay there or move somewhere else.

First, you need to see it and decide if you like it."

"Oh that sounds wonderful.

Of course I'll love Georgia...why wouldn't I if I'm there with you? And just where is this place you have in mind for a honeymoon?"

"That will be my little secret for now."

She nuzzled her head into his shoulder and asked nothing further. Any place in the world with him was bound to be perfect.

*

Their accommodations at Villa il Calle were perfect as before. The manager had personally greeted them and escorted them to the same suite that they had occupied on their first visit there together.

They spent a quiet evening following an in room dinner. Early the next morning, Maria suggested driving into town rather than taking a cab as they had traditionally done.

"It's a little quieter on Sunday.

There's a parking garage that I like to use just off the Lugarno del Tempio...that's the big street just ahead." She pointed to the intersection after crossing the Arno River into the antiquated section of town.

"It's a little expensive, but I feel my car is protected and it's close to most of the attractions that people come to see in the old sections of Firenze."

From the Lugarno del Tempio she exited onto the small street that led to the garage entrance. There she negotiated the Fiat into a small space adjacent to a stairwell reserved for compact cars. After assuring herself that she had locked the doors with her remote device, they set out on foot for a day of sightseeing.

As they made their way towards the exit, she stopped and looked back over her shoulder.

"Did you see something?" he asked Maria.

"I've had the feeling several times in the past few days that someone may be watching us. I didn't want to say anything though...I didn't want you to think that I'm...how do you say... paranoid?"

"Yes, very good. But why would anyone be following us?

And who could possibly know us or know that we would be here...or for that matter where we are going?

Why, we barely know where we are going more than a few hours or a day ahead of time."

"I'm sure you're right. It's probably just my imagination. Although, locals do focus on tourists to rob, especially Americans.

C'mon.

Let's go enjoy the day."

She grabbed his hand and paraded him like a teenager along the Arno River walk.

"We were a little farther down the river at the Uffizi and the Pitti Palace the last time we were here" she said, pointing westward along the river bank.

"Now that you see where we were before, we'll take some back streets to the Piazza Santa Croce. It's one of my favorite locations."

They walked the several blocks to the piazza where the church of Santa Croce sat on the east side of the square. Souvenir stands were set up around the periphery, but most stood empty. The day was pleasant but like many weekend days in the cooler time of the year, the piazza stood relatively devoid of tourists.

"Let's go into the church. I want to show you some of the most historical tombs in Florence."

Once again, he was awed by the interior of the edifice.

"It was begun in twelve hundred and ninety-four supposedly by St. Francis himself and remains the principal Franciscan church in Florence. It wasn't completed until fourteen hundred and forty-two when it was consecrated by Pope Eugene IV.

Don't you find it intriguing that each of these huge churches took over a hundred years to complete and the architects and original builders who started the projects knew they would never live to see the finished product?"

"I continue to wonder just how they built these magnificent buildings in those eras when they had no modern tools…and yet most of them have withstood the test of time, weather and natural disasters better than our modern structures.

I remember that earthquake that occurred in Mexico City several decades ago. Most of the buildings left standing were the older ones.

The new structures just crumbled.

I also marvel at your knowledge of your country!"

Maria smiled and held his arm tighter.

As they walked around the church, she pointed to the famous tombs including those of Galileo, Dante and Niccolo Machiavelli; towards the rear of the basilica was the large monument to Michelangelo designed by Vasari.

"I don't know what to say. Everything in my country is so 'young' by comparison. I love seeing the historic sites around Atlanta, but the city was only founded in eighteen hundred and thirty-seven.

Even our Civil War ended just a century and a half ago.

It's really a history lesson every place you go here."

Looking at a different section of the church referred to as the Niccolini Chapel, he read the plaque indicating that Giorgio Vasari had modernized the area for Cosimo di Medici between fifteen hundred and sixty-six and fifteen hundred and eighty-four.

"There's a mention of the Medicis again. I guess they were just such an integral part of everything that happened in the formative years of Florence."

"Why don't we find a café and have an espresso?" Maria suggested.

"We've been here almost two hours already and your feet must be getting a little tired like mine.

Then I want to take you to the Duomo. It's quite a walk so maybe we should get a taxi."

"I just love walking these old streets with you…if you're up to it?"

She demurred.

"We can take a taxi back to the garage."

Together they strolled to the nearest espresso café.

*

The walk to the Duomo was a bit longer than she remembered and that either had anticipated.

"Now my feet are really getting tired" Maria said.

"I should have worn flatter shoes. I should know better after all the time I've spent walking these streets."

"I can always put you over my shoulder and carry you if you like."

She laughed.

She was beginning to understand…and enjoy… his humor.

"Save that for the bedroom."

He laughed in turn.

"You're catching on to American slang.

I like that!"

They stood at the entrance to the very large edifice and stared at the top.

"Well, this is it…Santa Maria del Fiore…Saint Mary of the Flower, or **Duomo** as most people prefer to call it here.

That's Italian for cathedral."

This time Jack looked annoyed.

"You've told me that several times. I've got it."

Maria ignored his comment and continued.

"It was begun in twelve hundred and ninety-six. The main buildings minus the dome were completed by fourteen hundred and twenty after a lengthy series of architects were involved due to many untimely deaths.

In fourteen hundred and twenty a competition was held for the design and completion of the dome. Brunelleschi won the

89

competition and completed the world's only octagonal dome without a wooden supporting frame by fourteen hundred and thirty-six.

Come.

I want to show you the interior."

"You sound like a tour guide."

"I guess I forgot to mention that I was one for a while in Naples. And I've been here so many times that I tend to remember most of the facts and dates."

"Well, then, lead on."

After an exhaustive tour of all of the major components of the Duomo, they decided it was time to call it a day and return to the Villa il Calle for a rest before drinks and dinner.

They took a taxi back to the garage, secured her Fiat and paid the attendant as they exited.

Maria stared into the rear view mirror before moving out into traffic. She hesitated for several moments.

"Is something wrong?"

"It's the same face I've noticed behind us several times today. I'm convinced that whoever he is, he's following us."

"Get into the traffic quickly and make a few sudden turns. If he's interested in following us, he's welcome to try but we should be able to lose him fairly easily on these narrow winding streets.

Not that I doubt that you've seen someone both times today, but I seriously can't believe that anyone would be following us... despite what you said about tourists.

You don't have a jealous boyfriend somewhere that you didn't tell me about, do you?"

He smiled at her and she laughed in return as she stepped on the accelerator and pulled into the moderately heavy traffic along the Lugarno del Tempio heading toward the Arno River and the bridge that would take them back to the villa.

"There, I feel better already" Maria remarked as they passed over the river.

They couldn't know that a miniature transmitter had been placed behind the Fiat's rear bumper and that their every move was being monitored.

CHAPTER FOURTEEN

While the couple enjoyed a leisurely dinner in the gourmet dining room at Villa il Calle, they could not know that a team of professional thieves, sent by their American boss, stealthily scouted out their room while being careful not to leave any evidence of having been there.

They wore surgical gloves so that no finger prints would be left behind. The gloves were the highest quality talc free variety that left no residue that could be traced to a specific manufacturer should their presence in the room be detected and trace evidence searched for.

Their mission was to glean as much information about the couple as they could.

1) Why had Maria Rosato's male friend called Toto Catalano?
2) Just what was his relationship, if any, to the former Sicilian Mafia Don?
3) Was he a member of some rival gang?
4) And what was his exact relationship to the beautiful Maria Rosato?

The search appeared to be going nowhere. The team had examined the couple's personal articles contained within several pieces of luggage and found nothing of interest.

One of the trio, a computer specialist, accessed the personal files on Jack's laptop with ease and read the e-mail list and missives sent recently. There was nothing to suggest any sinister connections.

Perhaps it had all been just an honest mistake.

As they were preparing to leave, checking for any breach of security on their own part, one of the trio noticed a small tote bag containing the copy of a letter from someone named Thomas Catalano with an address in Philadelphia.

Significant?

Another of the team members carefully unfolded the missive and hurriedly photographed it using a miniature digital camera. There would be time later to examine its contents and submit it to the boss for his perusal and comment.

Alerted that the couple may be en route back to the room, they exited the suite ostensibly leaving it in the same pristine condition that they had found it.

*

After dinner, they retired to the bar lounge for an aperitif and a quiet chat about the next days activities. But Jack quickly brought the conversation back to their day in Florence.

"I can't help but be concerned about these people you seem to think are following us" he said to Maria.

"Is there any good reason to believe that someone would be following you...or me for that matter?"

"No, as I said earlier at the garage.

But, I have a sense about these things and it's often hard for me to shake a feeling once I get it. My late husband Paulo used to tease me about it, but he came to realize that when I got such a feeling, I was usually right about it.

It's just that it often takes quite a while for that reason to become apparent."

Jack extended his hand across the table as a reassuring gesture.

"I learned a long time ago never to underestimate the power of a woman's intuition. My mother was that way too. It took my father a long time to realize how right her hunches usually were.

They used to have lengthy arguments over her suspicions. But in the long run, he found that he had to...shall we say 'eat crow'?

Oops!

There's that puzzled look again.

It's another old American expression that means to admit you're wrong.

I'm going to try not to be that kind of husband" he said as he squeezed her hand and gazed into her dark brown eyes.

"That sounds nice...husband.

It will be so satisfying to call you husband, knowing that you will be there for me when I need comforting.

Now perhaps we should go back to the room and get comfortable?"

*

As they entered the room, one of those feelings instantly gripped her.

"Someone has been in here" she said authoritatively.

"Not that I would doubt you, but how can you tell?" he replied.

She walked around the room, inspecting it as she went. Walking into the bathroom, she hastily called to him and pointed to the sink area.

"A long time ago, when I first started getting these feelings, I made sure that I always left my cosmetics arranged in a certain way so that I could tell if anyone had moved them.

See!"

She pointed to a lipstick and a perfume bottle.

"I always leave the labels facing outward...these are now turned around. Most intruders wouldn't pay attention to such detail."

"I assure you I will never question you after this.

But once again, who would have done it and why?

And what do we do about it?"

She looked at him with a blank stare. It was obvious she didn't have a good answer either.

*

Maria convinced him begrudgingly that it would be best if they relocated to another hotel in case the answer to whoever was following them portended something more ominous than either could imagine at the moment.

For the time being, they would continue their search for Francesco Catalano and hope that the maid service at the Villa had just been tidying up the bathroom.

"This is all very frightening.

Just hold me tight."

The day's activities had left them both too tired to consider love making; instead, they found comfort in each other's arms and fell asleep that way.

The following morning, however, he was pleasantly aroused by Maria sitting astride him.

"I couldn't help but notice that you were dreaming of me" she said pointing to his erection.

"No reason to let a good thing go to waste."

He pulled her close as they rapidly coupled to each other.

"Now that's what I call a good morning wake-up call."

That puzzled look once more appeared on her face.

*

They had their belongings sent to the car while they shared breakfast. Then they relocated to downtown Florence.

Maria recommended a more central hotel to obviate the need for using her car in the crowded downtown area where parking was always a problem...and major expense. She had previously stayed at the Rivoli, situated adjacent to the Piazza Santa Maria Novella.

"Let me call the hotel and secure a room for later today. I'll only be a moment or two."

Excusing herself, she went to the lobby, made the reservation and then placed a second call.

"You'd better check on these people following us right away. Someone broke into our suite last night. I don't think they took anything, but get a crew over there right now and investigate it before the maids clean the room and destroy any possible evidence."

*

Returning to their breakfast table, she sat and sipped her coffee.

"Now, let's try to have a pleasant day…and I promise I will try **not** to find anyone else spying on us."

He nodded his agreement.

*

They arrived at the Rivoli hotel early in the day and had their bags moved to the holding area pending the availability of their room that was currently being cleaned. The valet handed her claim tickets for the luggage and car.

"Well, I guess it's time we got back down to business. It's too soon for lunch…although we could get an espresso if you like?"

"No, my dear Maria. I'm still full from breakfast.

Why don't we just get started with the job at hand? I'm anxious to see what we can find out about Francesco Catalano and the Medici.

We can worry about lunch later.

And just where would you suggest we begin?"

"There are two big libraries nearby: the **Biblioteca Medicea Laurenzia** and the **Biblioteca Nazionale Centrale**.

I would suggest we start with the Medicea Laurenzia…it's on the Piazza San Lorenzo… not far from here" she reassured him.

"Let's try not to wear out our shoes again today."

She smiled, remembering his comment from the day before.

"It's supposed to contain a wealth of information on the Medici family, including some documents taken from the Pitti Palace collection."

*

They arrived at the building's main entrance within ten minutes and made their way into the foyer.

"Here's a pamphlet with a brief history of the building" Maria remarked handing it to him.

"It was opened around fifteen hundred and seventy-one at the wish of Cosimo I de Medici in a setting designed by Michelangelo himself. Many of the original manuscripts contained here were donated from the Medici collection…among them those of

Sophocles and one of only three complete collections of **Plato's Dialogi**. It also houses an extensive collection of Egyptian papyri." He stopped reading the pamphlet and turned toward her.

"Well, that all sounds very interesting, but perusing those areas of history is not our current mission.

Why don't we just go directly to the reference room and see what they have about Ferdinando de Medici? Hopefully we can find notations about someone named Francesco Catalano among the articles written about him."

*

The couple labored for almost three days, poring over hundreds of papers, manuscripts and tomes from the fifteenth and sixteenth century before striking pure gold!

"Maria, look at this" he exclaimed.

"It says here that Ferdinando had briefly in his employ a young Italian named Francesco who was a student sent from southern Italy. He studied with him briefly, but decided to leave his tutelage and went to seek his own fortunes in **Campagna...in Salerno**!"

"Let me see that" she exclaimed.

"It's too much of a coincidence again not to be him. Is there no last name mentioned?"

He showed her the reference that he was examining.

"The young man named Francesco had come from somewhere in the southern regions of Italy. After being an apprentice for almost five years, he left following the death of his father who had come to be with him in his final days. He had helped Ferdinando establish banking concerns in numerous cities in the Tuscany and Campania regions."

"It' got to be him!

I think you've made the connection that you were hoping for. And can you believe it?...it's leading us right back to where we started!"

She put her arms around his neck and gave him a great big hug and kiss.

Patrons in nearby study carrels eyed the couple with looks suggesting that they were disturbingly out of place...as they clearly were.

"Shhh!" He admonished her.

"I don't care" she once again exclaimed.

"I'm sure you found what you've been looking for...and I don't care if they throw us out of here."

He smiled.

"You're right.

Whee!" he exclaimed enthusiastically in response.

"Let's collect our things and go celebrate.

Tomorrow, we go back home to Campagna to find Francesco Catalano!"

CHAPTER FIFTEEN

For almost half a century following his marriage to Lucretia Campanezzi, Francesco Catalano, known locally and throughout most...if not all of the lands that would collectively be called *Italy* following the *Risorgimento* of 1863...as *Il Padrino*, remained ensconced in the tiny village of Campagna...a site that offered him protection from the many enemies he had made as head of the largest protection organization in the Campania region and surrounding areas.

Lucretia lived a mere twenty years following their marriage during which time she remained faithful to the vow of silence made to her husband under duress on their wedding night. She found solace in the comfortable life he provided her and ultimately bore him twelve children, seven of whom survived to adulthood. Five of the surviving progeny were male children, ensuring that the lineage would continue for at least another generation.

Michele, the eldest, was heir to the vast family holdings at the time of Francesco's death in sixteen forty-nine. And in the manner that he had been so well tutored by his father, he established himself as a ruthless leader and neglectful husband.

And like his father, he sired five sons.

The dynasty would be safe through at least another generation.

*

Florence had been exciting and informative, but Jack and Maria were elated upon reaching Campagna and the thoughts of what might lie ahead in their quest for Francesco Catalano and his descendants.

The following morning, they returned to the local museum to see if there was any information available specifically on Francesco Catalano, not having known about him on the initial visit.

An older woman named Concetta Dedario had assumed the position formerly held by Maria at the museum. While the two women had met previously, they were not particularly well acquainted.

"***Buon giorno***" Maria began, not being sure how much English the woman was comfortable with.

"Good morning" she replied in acceptable English.

"I hope you remember me? I'm Maria Rosato."

"Yes. I remember you. People ask for you all the time" she quickly answered.

She leaned forward to give Maria a hug. After introductions were made, Maria came right to the point concerning the purpose of their visit.

As they stood in the entrance vestibule, Jack suddenly found himself looking at the portrait of a young man who appeared to be in his late twenties or early thirties hanging on the entrance wall. The subject's clothing suggested that it was from the sixteenth or seventeenth century.

"Excuse me, Concetta, but would you happen to know anything about this painting?

I don't remember seeing it the last time I was here.

Maria, you used to work here. Do you recognize it?"

She turned to face the portrait.

"That is new since I left here. I don't remember seeing it before.

Would you know where it came from?" she asked Concetta.

"I have only worked here for a few weeks. I think that someone from the mayor's office donated it with the stipulation that the museum agree to hang it where it could be in full view of the patronage."

He walked closer to examine the small plaque at the bottom of the frame. It identified the person only as ***Il Padrino.***

"How does that translate?" he queried the two Italian women.

"I think you would call him *'Godfather'*, much like the title of your famous American movie."

"Is there any more information on exactly who he is...I mean his real name or when he lived?"

She shrugged a "no".

"We could take the picture off the wall and see if there is anything attached to the back."

They were all disappointed that the reverse side of the framing was bare.

"Well, then perhaps we need to talk to whomever donated it from the mayor's office. Perhaps they can shed some light on it for us."

Once again Maria gazed at him with a bewildered look.

Again he laughed.

"It means maybe they know something about it that will enlighten us."

She smiled and shook her head, acknowledging that she now understood.

*

The mayor's office was in a small, unremarkable building situated in the middle of a block of attached two-story structures on the narrow curving main street of Campagna. There were two rooms on the ground floor. The outer room was occupied by a secretary who appeared to be in her seventies. A small name plate on her desk identified her only as Rosa.

Maria engaged her in conversation in Italian since it was obvious from the woman's first utterances that she neither spoke nor understood English.

After what seemed to him to be a rather lengthy conversation, of which he understood virtually nothing, Maria turned to him.

"She said that it was a gift from an old nearby estate. Apparently the last remaining member of the family died recently. In addition to the portrait, they left the city a substantial sum of money to be used to fund the building of a new museum for genealogy research and the arts.

Hanging the portrait in the entrance of the museum was one of the stipulations of the bequest."

"I guess I'd hang it in the doorway too if someone gave me money along with it," he remarked in a casual manner.

"Just how much money are we talking about?"

Maria turned to the woman and posed the question in Italian.

"A quarter of a million Euros!"

He almost choked on her words as he attempted to calculate the amount in his head.

"Why that's about two hundred and eighty thousand U.S. dollars at the current exchange rate.

Whoever left it to the city must have been very wealthy and had good reason to leave it to such a small town. Is there anyone else that could help us find out about the benefactor?"

Once more Maria turned and spoke to Rosa in Italian.

"She says that she is sure that the mayor can tell us who is the executor of the estate...but he is out of town until tomorrow so we'll have to come back then."

He acknowledged her help by nodding to the old woman and uttering one of the few words that he knew in her language.

"Grazie."

*

After breakfast the following morning, they returned to the mayor's office where they were pleased to be introduced to his honor, Antonio Badalementi. Thankfully, he was fluent in English.

"Your honor, we are interested in the painting that was recently placed in the entrance to the museum. What can you tell us about it?"

"Please, my friends call me Antonio.

We were blessed with a large donation from the trust of the late Angelo Gibboni. In addition to that painting and several others from the same era, there was a substantial amount of cash involved. It will allow us to construct a new museum with a more appropriate visitor's center. We are only beginning to formulate plans for such a project, but we hope to have represented genealogical records for all the town's inhabitants, past and present, as well as any we can obtain from Salerno province and Campania.

For quite a number of years now we have been getting inquiries from all over the world for such information. Your country really awakened interest in genealogy several decades ago with the T.V.

mini-series 'Roots', and then more recently with the Ellis Island project.

The internet has made even small towns like mine very popular. But it takes a good deal of money to be able to respond to such requests...and to provide meaningful information."

"I'm impressed that you know so much about America."

"I try to keep informed of what is going on around the world as well as in Campania.

Now, I didn't know Angelo Gibboni very well. But, I understand that he has some relatives somewhere in Naples as well as in the United States...in New York or Connecticut, I believe."

"It may be just a coincidence, Antonio, but that's where my grandparents were from. They started in New York in the late eighteen hundreds and then moved to Connecticut at the beginning of the twentieth century.

That name...Gibboni...sounds vaguely familiar. I think one of my ancestors was named that, but I'll need to do more research on it.

Do you think you can find out where the relatives are in Naples?"

"I'll see what I can do and have Concetta call you."

"By the way, Antonio, do you have any idea who '*Il Padrino*' was?"

Antonio looked puzzled for a moment.

"Oh! You mean the painting in the museum entrance?

I think it has something to do with one of the Gibboni's ancestors. That's one of the things we hope to resolve with our new research tools."

The couple thanked him for his time and made their way to the Fiat parked just outside the office. As they approached it, Maria gazed down the street.

"Wait. Let's take a walk to the church", she suggested.

"I haven't been in there in years. I somehow remember seeing a number of old paintings in the basement. Many are religious, I'm sure. But if my memory serves me well, there were some that looked similar to the one in the museum.

Perhaps there is a connection."

He was happy to take her hand and leisurely walk the almost deserted streets of Campagna where it appeared that time had frozen a century or two ago.

They found their way down the well worn steps to the rather dingy and musty smelling church basement. It housed the social hall and several smaller rooms apparently used as guest accommodations for visiting priests and dignitaries.

"The door to this room is open" she said, as she disappeared into the semi-darkened space.

Suddenly, she gasped.

He quickly followed to see what she had found.

The natural light from the single weather and dirt stained window allowed him to make out a rather large portrait of a man in garb similar to the one at the museum.

He found a switch next to the door frame and turned on the light.

On the adjacent wall hung the portrait of a man that bore a striking resemblance to the subject of the painting at the museum...and dressed in clothing that suggested they were from the same era.

At the bottom of the frame was a small name plate engraved with "*Il Coltello*".

"What on earth does that mean?" he queried.

"Coltello means knife in Italian."

"So we have what appears to be the same person in the two paintings with one called 'The Knife' and the other called 'Godfather'.

I'm sure there must be an interesting story there somewhere.

Now, all we need to do is find out what it is."

CHAPTER SIXTEEN

"Well, so far you have found out exactly nothing... nothing!" he exclaimed through the speaker phone to the small band of men that he had follow the couple around the center of Firenze and later search their room at Villa il Calle.

The men let him vent his anger. They knew better than to try to make excuses for their lack of results. As he continued his ranting, they could only sit and listen.

"I will give you only one more chance to find out what they are really doing there. That gentleman did not come all the way from America simply to look up an ancestor...he and that woman must be on to something having to do with me or else why would they have traveled all over Italy to most of my ancestors present and former homes.

Surely, they must be looking to expose me.

Now, get going and find out the truth!"

As echoes of the angered voice lingered, there followed a loud thud as the phone was slammed into its cradle.

The men left without uttering another word to one another.

Action and results were the only things that the boss understood.

*

Michele Catalano proudly assumed the role of *Il Padrino* upon his father's death, emulating him in every way...especially in his ruthlessness, now the trademark of the Catalanos of Campagna.

The façade of the banking business, now entering its fourth decade in the Campania area, continued to make him and his partners respectable inhabitants of the region. However, knowledge of the protection scheme and other illicit businesses that emanated from it continued to circulate across the years.

Unlike his father, Michele made no plans for marriage until well into his forties when he was presented the opportunity to acquire additional lands adjacent to the neighboring town of Eboli by his marriage to the chief merchant's daughter.

"*Il Padrino*" the young lady's father began, "you would honor my family by accepting the hand of my youngest daughter, Giovanna, in marriage. Her dowry to you will be half of my lands that extend between our two villages."

"Don Ferrara, that is most generous…and hardly necessary considering how beautiful your daughter is. She hardly needs so generous a dowry to find a man willing to accept her as his wife."

He stood holding the man at bay for a few moments.

"But I will accept your gracious offer. The women, I'm sure, will be more than happy to see to the details of the wedding."

"You make me a happy man, *Il Padrino*. I am at your service this day and for all days to come."

And so it would go generation after generation until the time of Italian reunification…the Campania region continued to be dominated by succeeding generations of Catalano first born men, each of whom were only too happy to accept the title of *Il Padrino* or simply *"Godfather"*.

*

Following the discovery of the painting in the church basement that bore a striking resemblance to the one now prominently displayed in the town museum, the couple hurried back to the mayor's office.

After explaining to him about their astonishing find, they enquired into the feasibility of obtaining permission to examine the estate of the deceased patron, Angelo Gibboni.

"I will be pleased to see what can be arranged. As you would say in your country, there is a lot of 'red tape' involved in arranging such matters due to the fact that there are no immediate relatives that we have identified and the matter lies with the courts and the city council.

I am sure that you are aware that the legal system in my country is not known for the speed at which it operates…in fact, just the opposite."

Everyone laughed heartedly in appreciation of understanding fully the mayor's statement.

His sense of humor made them all relax as they discussed how to resolve the situation.

"I will talk to the chief magistrate at the court house tomorrow and see if I can arrange for us to tour the estate and see what other useful bits of information we might discover about him… and possibly about your family.

Since it is lunch time, may I offer to host you at the trattoria nearby on our main street? It will be at the city's pleasure."

"How can one turn down such a generous offer from a city official?" Maria answered for the couple.

"Thank you Mr. Mayor…Antonio. We accept."

*

Following lunch with the mayor, Maria requested that his honor accompany them back to the church so that he might see the painting that they had discovered.

"I'm sure at some time I must have seen the art work in the church…but I somehow don't remember it. If there is a relationship between the Gibboni painting that is now in the museum and the one in the church, I have no recollection of it."

It was a short walk between the trattoria and the church and the trio arrived there in a matter of minutes.

"Well, there it is" Maria announced as they entered the basement room.

Antonio stood and surveyed the painting for a moment or two and then turned toward the couple.

"You are quite right! I think the two are one and the same… or certainly related…although painted at different times. The subject in this one appears ten or twenty years older than the other."

And then turning toward Jack, he said:

"And do you not think that these two subjects bear a striking resemblance to you?"

Maria interjected her thoughts first.

"I thought that myself, but somehow I was reluctant to suggest it." She turned toward him for his answer to the mayor's question.

"Yes." He replied.

"My God!

These must be relatives of mine!"

PART THREE

CHAPTER SEVENTEEN

The year was eighteen sixty-six and for over three centuries the Catalano first born males had succeeded in carrying on the family tradition as *Il Padrino*. Based in the tiny mountainous village of Campagna, each heir to the title had managed to terrorize not only the Campania region, but had earned a country wide reputation for the fear that each successive gangs of thugs had inflicted on the populace in general.

Michele, the current would be successor, knew that the coming of Risorgimento would surely sound the death knell for him and his people, as the leaders assuming power of the now united country of Italy had made abundantly clear to him and gangs like his that they would no longer be tolerated. His father had decided that any future progeny would not be made to suffer for the "sins of the fathers."

Accordingly, he had disbanded his gang and was content to be only the banker and legal advisor to the city of Campagna that his predecessors had purported to be for centuries before him.

Michele had married Agostina Gibboni ten years earlier. She had borne him three young girls; her first pregnancy had been a male child who had died soon after birth.

On the first of May of the same year, eighteen sixty-six, she gave birth to a healthy son, Felice. He grew to manhood strong and proud of his Italian heritage. However, from the time that he first became aware of his family's place of power in the region, it was instilled in him that *Il Padrino* was a term of the past. The title had ended with his grandfather and the family prepared to leave their native country for America or suffer the consequences of the coming governmental reorganization.

Plans were being formulated for the family's emigration in the near future...or sooner if deemed absolutely necessary. In the meantime, the family sought refuge wherever possible.

*

"Mi Amor", Michele whispered to Agostina, "the time has come for you to take the children and leave for New York. It is becoming too unsafe here. It will be best for you and the children that we travel alone in case I am stopped.

But, I will keep Felice with me so that hopefully I will appear like just a normal married man traveling with his child."

The family had been forced for almost twenty years to remain in hiding in various parts of southern Italy, protected by members of their former gang.

Through a variety of connections both within Italy and in America, passage had been arranged and documents had been prepared for their escape. Though they maintained the family name, their occupations, places of birth and cities of origin had been tailored.

Agostina would depart with her remaining six children on the ship **Cheribon** that was scheduled to sail from Naples to New York. During the final five years of their hiding out at her father's estate near Campagna, she had been blessed with three additional sons.

*

Their departure had been delayed for several days. But finally, on May 16, 1892, after a frightful ten days at sea, Agostina and her children set eyes on their new home country for the first time.

Arriving at Ellis Island, she gathered up the children and led them along with her fellow passengers to the waiting authorities and the screening process that she and the others found brutal. The lines were long, the waiting times longer still, and the smaller children became frightened when being poked and prodded or being asked to undress in front of strangers. Fortunately, the entire family's health was good and only two days after debarking the

Cheribon, they were granted entrance into the city of New York, gateway to their new life in America.

Arrangements for them to be met and escorted to a home in upper Manhattan were accomplished with a minimum of inconvenience. There they would await the arrival of Michele and Felice.

*

Things were far more problematic for Michele and Felice since recognition by the authorities was a constant threat. Michele grew a beard and young Felice, now twenty-six, attempted to hide his normal facial features with a thick moustache and eyeglasses. Both wore wide brim hats to shadow their facial features.

Naples, the main port of debarkation to America from Italy, was replete with officials looking for criminals attempting to escape the country. Accordingly, Michele had his contacts arrange transportation for the pair to Messina, on the island of Sicily...just across the straits that bore the same name and opposite the "boot" of Italy... with their final destination the port city of Palermo. From there, they would arrange passage to whichever American port was the least hazardous.

The journey to Palermo was treacherous physically due to the ruggedness of the terrain crossed, and equally exhausting mentally with the constant threat of being discovered by the Italian authorities.

Though it had been a decade or more since Michele had disappeared from view, he remained a high priority fugitive on the new Italian government's list of wanted criminals.

Having reached Cefalu, approximately half way between the two cities, Michele was made aware of the presence of a large force of officials in Palermo looking to arrest him and his son and return them to Campania to face charges.

"My son, I'm sorry but we're going to have to remain here until it is safe again in Palermo. My men are continuing to monitor the situation and will let us know the proper time to proceed."

Neither father nor son expected almost two years to elapse before such clearance would be given. Michele arranged for them to learn English during the interlude, gambling that this would help in their ability to clear customs on arrival in America as well as speed up their transition to citizenship.

Felice was apprenticed to an older gentleman barber who agreed to teach him his trade, again providing him with a real and honest "occupation" when they finally reached America and registered for citizenship.

It was the last day of September, 1895 when *La Bretagne*, a French steamer, entered the harbor of New Orleans with four hundred and eight passengers on board, mostly Italians from Sicily. Included on the passenger manifest were the names of Felix and Michael Catalonia. Hopefully their new names would help them clear customs more easily. After the ship had been given clearance by medical authorities, the passengers were directed to customs where Michele was approached by an inspector. He steeled himself for the worst.

Instead, the inspector directed his remarks toward Felice and made no mention of their names.

"I see from your papers that you spent time in service in the Italian militia, and that you list your current occupation as a barber.

Being a former military man myself, I congratulate you, sir.

And what are your plans here in America?"

"Sir, if at all possible, I would like to have my own barber shop here in the New Orleans area. We have some acquaintances who have agreed to help us make a start."

"You both speak very good English."

"We were fortunate to have spent time with acquaintances that had lived in America and spoke the language well. We knew it would be helpful to learn the language before we arrived."

"Then I wish you both success."

He stamped their papers and allowed them to make their way from the docks into the heart of the city.

"That went well. I was afraid he was on to us by his approach. Putting the militia service into your records was a brilliant move. People in uniform seem to love others who have worn one. It's a good thing they don't have a way to document it.

And learning to speak English helped as I had been assured it would.

Now, one more thing my son. Our name changes have to be permanent.

From now on, I'm will call you 'Felix'. And you are to refer to me as 'Michael' when you are asked for my name. But call me Dad or Pop otherwise. That sounds more American."

The pair obviously had no intentions of staying in New Orleans. Rather, they would make their way to New York by the quickest means possible. It had been a long time since they had seen their family and both were anxious to reunite with them and start their new lives in America.

CHAPTER EIGHTEEN

Maria suggested another excursion into Naples since there were numerous parts of the city that they had not explored...in fact, their earlier trip had barely scratched the surface. There was no rationale for sitting around the small town of Campagna while the mayor and the necessary court officials determined if they could legally inspect the Gibboni estate.

"The mayor has my cell phone number" Maria remarked.

"So, let's just go and enjoy the city. If we have time, we can visit Pompeii or the Amalfi coast if you like...of course, not all in one day. I think we should pack a suitcase and plan to stay until the mayor calls us."

"That sounds great to me" he replied.

"I've seen so little of the major tourist sites, thanks to chasing our tail from Campagna to southern Italy and back."

There was that look again on Maria's face.

"Chasing our tail?

Just what does that mean?"

"Did you ever watch a dog or cat going around in a circle chasing its own tail?

Well, that's sort of what we did in tracking down my relatives. We started out in Campagna, got some clues and then went to Spain, Florence, Catanzaro, Vibo Valentia, Florence again and finally back here.

Chasing our tail."

She smiled.

"Now I understand.

You Americans do have some very quaint and colorful ways of saying things."

She reached up and kissed him lightly on the lips.

"But that's just one more reason why I love you."

He responded by quickly sweeping her off her feet, lifting her over his shoulder and carrying her into the bedroom where he threw her onto the bed. She laughed as she bounced a time or two.

"Come here, I have something I want to show you."

He dived onto the bed.

"And I have something here that I want to show you as well."

*

"Show and tell" delayed their departure by about two hours.

"Now" he said as they put their things into her car.

"It's going to be a good day, no matter what else happens."

Maria nodded her concurrence.

*

The road from Eboli towards Naples took them past the turnoff to the Amalfi peninsula.

"Why don't we drive the Amalfi coast road first?

It's such a beautiful day and I think you will agree after you've driven it that it is one of the most scenic places in all the world."

"You're driving" he said, nodding his agreement.

She skillfully guided the Fiat from the A3 towards Amalfi. The coast road is famous for stunning views of the Tyrrhenian Sea from its heights as well as the Isle of Capri off its western end and Mount Vesuvius to the north. Its proximity to Herculaneum and Pompeii and several other ancient Roman towns makes it a good jumping off point for day trips from any of its famous and exquisitely beautiful towns and villages.

In miles traveled, the distances between towns along the coast are short. But the winding road and the constant need to stop at vista points to view the scenery made the journey take much longer than he would have imagined, not being familiar with the geography. Maria was so thoroughly familiar with the route she could have been a professional tour guide.

"This is the Costiera Amalfitana...just one part of my native Campania...but certainly one of the best known and most frequently visited.

Just over there a few miles is Ravello. Like most Italian cities, it has a Duomo, famous for its 'Pulpit of the Gospels' designed by Nicolo Bartolomeo in 1272."

She continued her narrative as she drove.

He looked at his watch, noted the time and then finally broke the silence.

"You know, I don't think we're really going to get any where near to Naples any time soon. Perhaps we should consider spending the night in one of these wonderful little villages."

"I was hoping you would suggest that" Maria answered.

"Actually, I was counting on it. I have a favorite hotel in the village of Amalfi."

"Let me guess...you've been here a hundred times before and they probably know you by your first name much like the manager at Villa il Calle?"

Maria laughed.

"I guess you're beginning to know me too well.

Perhaps not a hundred times...let's just say many. When you travel in certain businesses and you spend a moderate amount of money, people tend to remember you.

My late husband's business was one of those."

He let that thought linger for a few moments.

"What's the name of this hotel?"

"The Santa Caterina."

"I suppose it's a four star hotel?"

"Five star."

"Was your husband *that* wealthy?"

Jack hesitated as he realized that he was delving into her very personal life. But perhaps it was time to learn some facts about Paulo.

"I shouldn't have said that" he quickly added.

"No. No. It's all right.

Now that we're engaged, you have a right to know all about me and my past.

We haven't really talked all that much about Paulo...or anything about my personal finances.

Let's just say that he left me fairly 'well off'. I enjoy the finer things in life since I am able to.

And that includes you, my *dolce*."

"Thank you."

*

The entrance to the hotel was no less stunning than he would have expected...gray stone with horizontal fluting and a large glass canopy protecting the entrance. The flooring of the lobby was Italian marble, with Greek Corinthian columns adorning and partitioning the vast expanse of space; the rear of the lobby opened onto a terrace that featured a Mediterranean blue water pool that segued onto the white sand beach along the Tyrrhenian Sea.

"Well, if this is what the lobby looks like", he commented, "I can't wait to see the room you've chosen."

Maria turned and cast a gaze his way that told him his words had not been appreciated.

"Sorry" he whispered as the desk clerk approached.

"Ah! Nice to see you again, Mrs. Rosato. Will Mr. Rosato be joining us later?"

She explained to the clerk how her husband had suddenly passed away, taking care not to offend her for asking.

She then introduced her fiancé to the clerk and asked if her 'usual' room was available?

"This is your lucky day. It was occupied, but the gentleman and his wife had an emergency that necessitated their returning to Rome urgently. They left just a short while ago.

May I recommend that you and the gentleman have a complimentary cocktail on the terrace while we prepare your room?"

"That is most kind."

As she turned toward Jack, he nodded in the affirmative.

"I will have the bellman take your things to the suite and your waiter will notify you as soon as everything is ready.

Will you be having dinner with us this evening?

I'd be happy to see that your favorite table is reserved."

"Yes. That's most kind of you…. I'm sorry. I've forgotten your name."

"Forgive me, Mrs. Rosato.

It's Isabella."

"Well then thank you, Isabella."

The couple moved off to the terrace where they found a table offering the most spectacular view he had ever seen. The table held a large umbrella in its center to protect patrons from the sun.

"Everyone on the terrace seems to be staring at you. Do you know any of them?"

"It's the Sophia Loren thing. It's rare to go anywhere in my country without people either staring or coming up and asking for autographs."

The waiter had just taken their drink order when Maria suddenly jumped up and ran toward an approaching woman of about seventy. They hugged and kissed each other's cheeks.

"This is my fiancé" she said, and then turned toward him.

"This is Ninni Gambardella. Her grandfather built the original hotel here in the eighteen eighties. Then her parents ran it until they turned it over to Ninni and her sister, Giusi."

"I am so pleased to meet you" she said as she took his hand.

Turning to Maria she whispered privately.

"I'm so sorry to hear about your husband's death. Isabella told me that you had arrived and confided the information to me about his passing."

She then turned back toward Jack.

"Is this your first time to Amalfi?"

"Yes."

"It will be dusk soon. You haven't lived until you've seen a sunset over the Tyrrhenian Sea."

"I'm beginning to think I hadn't lived at all before coming to your country!"

*

"Does the man sitting three tables over along the edge of the terrace look familiar to you?"

He turned his head slightly to see who it was that Maria was referring to.

"I don't think so.

Why?"

"He reminds me of one of the people we saw near the garage in Florence."

He shook his head in disbelief.

"How can you remember people's faces when you saw them at a distance for only a fraction of a second?

Not to mention, it's been quite a while since that day."

"It's one of my special talents" she replied.

The waiter interrupted to inform them that their suite was ready.

"You have some other special talents that I'd like to check out... in private of course.

Shall we go to our room?"

"You make me blush."

She took his offered hand and followed him into the lobby where the elevator to the concierge floor was waiting.

CHAPTER NINETEEN

Felix and Michael exited New Orleans immediately after they had been cleared by customs. They were eager to reach New York and be reunited with the family that they had not seen in several years.

They initially considered walking the distance. But, as they came to realize the enormity of America, the pair quickly fathomed the impracticality of a journey of that magnitude on foot. Their remaining funds were small, but adequate enough to spend a portion of it to hasten their journey home.

The river boats from New Orleans to St. Louis offered them their best option. From St. Louis, they could take a train directly to New York City and arrive at their destination in ten days or less.

They bought passage on the "*Mississippi Gambler*" departing two days following their debarkation in New Orleans. After a one day layover in St. Louis, they proceeded to New York City, arriving at their ultimate destination just eight days later after a host of intermediate stops.

They found the country's scenery engaging, although the portions they traversed were quite different than their homeland. Their major dislike so far was being called "WOPS" numerous times by strangers they encountered on their sojourn east.

"If we were back home, they would feel the wrath of *Il Padrino*" Michael whispered to Felix.

He was somewhat surprised at his father's viciousness since he had not witnessed any hostility while growing up in Italy. But then, he remembered that Michael had always been in charge. When he reminisced about stories told him concerning his grandfather and earlier generations of Catalano men, he could see why no one had challenged his father and why it had never been necessary for him to display aggression towards those in his employ.

When they arrived in the city, Michael had been instructed by his men in Palermo to go to the Little Italy section of the city and find Lombardi's restaurant. From there, they would be contacted and taken to the residence where the remaining members of the family anxiously awaited their return.

The bartender at Lombardi's immediately recognized the name and kissed *Il Padrino's* hand.

"We thought you and your son were never going to arrive. Giuseppe will take you to your family. Please be seated and enjoy a grappa while I send for him."

Michael felt that he was once again home.

*

Giuseppe arrived about thirty minutes later and greeted the pair.

"Your family lives in a home about a fifteen minute walk from here. Please follow me."

Agostina was on the bottom porch of the three story wooden frame home as the pair approached. At her sight, husband and son broke into a run.

"Oh, it's so good to see you both" she said, tears streaming down both cheeks. They stood holding one another so tightly, each could hardly breathe.

"Let me look at you" Agostina said, looking at her son.

"You've grown taller, and you look so handsome with the moustache...just like your father."

Michael smiled.

"And you my lovely wife, you look as beautiful as ever. I don't think you have aged a day since I last saw you.

We both have missed you so much."

Agostina blushed.

"Come. Let us not stand here where everyone can see and hear us. Let me get you something to eat and drink...you must be starved?"

"Would it be too much to ask for some pasta with that special sauce only you can make?"

"It's already made and waiting. We were alerted that you were on your way. Now you two go clean up before we eat."

Felix smiled at his mother.

"Some things never change."

＊

She handed each of her men a glass of campari as they gathered around the dining room table as a whole family for the first time in years. The table was large enough to accommodate a dozen people when extensions were added. A sideboard held a complete set of dishes and silverware.

"It's so good to taste the taste of home" Michael stated. "And such a lovely room this is. Quite different and elaborate compared to our home back in Italy."

For the next two hours over dinner, the family members listened as each side updated the other on all the events that had occurred during their time apart. Agostina and the children told of their adventures on the trip from Naples to New York and of their unpleasant experience at Ellis Island.

But their stories paled in comparison to those of Michael and Felix. Everyone listened intently as the pair told of their harrowing trip across the Messina Straits, of the time spent in Cefalu where they learned to speak English, and their trip to America and the boat and train journey from New Orleans to New York.

Everyone had questions about New Orleans and their journey on the Mississippi River and the train trip from St. Louis. Agostina had heard about these places during the time in New York waiting for her husband and son to return, but had never met anyone who had actually been there or experienced these things firsthand.

"And now" Michael added.

"We must be careful where we go and who we talk to. And we will change our names to the American versions. From now on, you will call me Michael or Mike, and our son here Felix or better yet, Freddie.

And you my lovely wife, we will call you Agnes...although I still prefer to call you 'Mama'.

And now, the day has been long and everyone must be tired, so let us continue our stories tomorrow after a good nights sleep."

Michael stood behind his wife's straight back chair and whispered to her that he was looking forward to their first night together after so long a time.

"Italian men never change!" she quietly replied so that only he could hear.

She smiled demurely as they made their way to the master bedroom.

"But then, Italian women wouldn't want them to", she added as she quickly closed the door and began to undress.

*

Jack and Maria were taken by elevator to the concierge level where the bellman led them to the Follia Amalfitana Suite, immersed in the delicate aroma of the nearby lemon and orange groves. Its many spectacular features included a shell shaped bed, emerald green ceramic tile floors contrasting dramatically to the white walls of the suite, and a sunken Jacuzzi on the terrace with a commanding view of the Gulf of Salerno, waters that were a part of the Tyrrhenian Sea to the west.

"It's more beautiful than anything I've ever seen in America or anywhere that I've traveled...and I've done a lot.

Were you trying to hide all this from me?

I mean, I thought the villa near Florence was nice...but this!"

She moved in closer to his side and rested her head against his shoulder.

"I assure you, my intentions were honorable.

You see, with my resemblance to someone beautiful and famous, and the fortune that I inherited when my husband died, I needed to be careful about whom I fell in love with. But now I know that you are here for me alone. I realize that you knew nothing about my personal life before you met me."

He peered into her eyes...and into her soul.

"I have never met anyone like you before.

And I'll never need to meet anyone again.

You fulfill all my needs."

"And you mine", Maria responded.

They kissed deeply as he led her to the shell shaped bed where they consummated their pledges to one another.

*

Since they couldn't know when to expect a call from Mayor Badalementi, they decided not to impose any time table on their activities, rather just relax and enjoy Amalfi and the surrounding coastal communities.

Amalfi, the town, was amazing...from its earliest history with references dating to the sixth century; to its introduction of maritime laws adopted by most of its seafaring neighbors in the eighth century; to its conquest by the Normans in the eleventh century and by several Italian city states during the Middle Ages. But perhaps their most interesting find was something totally unexpected: the burial place of the relics of St. Andrew. According to legend, the remains of the apostle saint were brought to Amalfi in the year twelve hundred and six from Constantinople by Pietro, Cardinal of Capua. The remains were entombed in the town's Duomo, named in honor of the saint. A statue of St. Andrew, sculpted by a pupil of Michelangelo, stands within the edifice.

Leaving the cathedral, they walked a narrow street towards the lido and stopped for gelato as they had done in Naples. They sat at a table fronting the sea.

"You know, I could get used to your lifestyle...if I didn't think it necessary that I work.

But tell me, after your mother passed away, what made you choose to stay in a small town like Campagna if this is more what you're used to?"

"There's more to life than money...although as most people who have it would confess...it helps. But after my husband"... tears formed in the corner of her eyes, but she managed to hold them back... "after Paulo died, I was so alone and needed to have something to take my mind off my personal problems during the day. It's important to me to stay in contact with people. It helps make me appreciate what I have even more. So the job at the museum was a perfect fit for the time.

And look what happened!

While I was feeling lonely and wondering just what I wanted to do with the rest of my life, you walked in.

And now you have given my life purpose again.

And all this is so much more fun when you share it with someone you love."

He reached for her hand.

"You can trust me when I say that our love will last forever."

She responded by holding his hand more tightly.

After a brief interlude during which neither one spoke, she stood.

"Let's drive to Positano...it's not far and you'll love the scenery. And we can take a walk on the beach."

*

The drive to Positano was short...by miles... along the winding, narrow and incredibly scenic coast line. Yet it took almost two hours during which time he reminisced about his good fortune as he gazed at the passing scenery.

When they arrived he again was amazed at the charm of the small town built on a hillside overlooking the waters of the Gulf of Salerno.

She parked the Fiat along the beach walk and they stepped onto the sand.

"Let's take our shoes off" Maria shouted, already holding one in her hand. She removed the other quickly and began running along the beach parallel to the water's edge.

He followed her lead, quickly caught up to her and took her hand. As they walked, the waves sprayed the cool water onto their bare feet.

"This is absolutely magnificent. And I thought places like Savannah beach and some of the Florida resort settings were exciting...but nothing like this.

Hawaii comes a little closer by comparison...but your country and this place in particular outdo them all."

"I'm glad you love Italy...and that it's all or more than you expected it to be."

The sounds of lapping waves were suddenly interrupted by the ringing of a cell phone.

Maria reached into her pocket and retrieved one of the smallest cell phones he had seen.

"Pronto" she said.

After a brief conversation...all in Italian...she replaced the phone into her pocket.

"I had left my number with the mayor...Antonio.

He has cleared it with all the necessary people for us to tour the Gibboni estate."

"That's great. But do we have to leave right away? I mean, as much as I want to find out what might be at the estate, I want to spend time alone with you even more."

She flashed her famous Gioconda smile his way.

"We will do it the Italian way...one day at a time and slowly."

*

"We've been following them just as you requested.

There's nothing to report so far. They're been staying in Amalfi and just sightseeing along the coastline. This Maria lady must have a lot of money, considering the hotels they have chosen. I'm reasonably sure he can't afford places like the Santa Caterina... rooms there can cost five hundred Euros or more a night.

We spent over fifty Euros apiece just for dinner and a drink while tailing them."

"That's O.K. I'm paying for everything.

Just let me know if anything changes."

CHAPTER TWENTY

Maria had contacted Mayor Antonio Badalementi in Campagna to advise him that they wouldn't be back in town for the better part of a week, and that she would call him upon their return.

He assured her that he would arrange complete access for them to the Gibboni estate at the couple's convenience.

With that communiqué taken care of, they were free to enjoy the Amalfi area and beyond. The business of the subjects of the paintings back home could wait until another day...one that would follow a leisurely holiday in one of Italy's most scenic and historic areas.

After two luxurious nights at the Santa Caterina, they decided... partly based on the fact that their suite needed to be vacated due to a prior booking...that they would move on to Sorrento and the Isle of Capri; make a brief stop at Pompeii; spend a day or two sightseeing in Naples and then return to Campagna.

She guided the Fiat along the spectacularly scenic laden highway SS163 past Positano, further along the shoreline until the road began the long and winding climb across the Lattari mountains. After intersecting SS145, they turned westward for the additional short drive into Sorrento.

"I'll just bet you know someone here that runs a fancy hotel... and at your sight will suddenly have a room available."

His subtlety was obvious.

"It just so happens...."

He laughed loudly.

He took her right hand and held it tightly.

"As I said before, I could learn to love this lifestyle."

*

She adroitly guided the car through the ancient and narrowed streets of downtown Sorrento. As they approached the bay side, she steered the car into the entrance driveway of the Parco Del Principi hotel, hanging on the side of a cliff with its terrace facing the Bay of Naples. Mount Vesuvius loomed large in the distance, faint in the haze of approaching dusk.

After registering, the couple was shown to their suite, which provided much the same view as from the terrace, but with the addition of several stories of height. As darkness increased, the glowing lights of Naples and the other cities along the bay illuminated the skyline.

"Not bad. Not bad!" was all he could say.

"Well, if you don't like it we can always...."

He stopped her in mid-sentence.

Standing behind her with his arms wrapped around her waist, he laid his chin on her shoulder.

"Nothing you could do would ever *not* please me.

This is magnificent...just magnificent.

Every time I think there can't be a more spectacular place in this country of yours, you take me to one better...or at least equally impressive.

This view of Naples and Vesuvius with the bay in between is like looking at a picture post card.

In fact, everywhere I glance is like another post card."

"I'm so glad that you like it here. Maybe we should consider living in my country after we are married?"

"I think the solution to that would be to have homes in both of our countries...although with my Italian heritage, it probably wouldn't take much to convince me to spend most of our time here."

She just purred in his arms as they stood and enjoyed the incomparable view.

*

"Boss, it looks like they're just on a sightseeing trip. Do you want us to continue following?"

"Go back home since we can monitor where they are at all times. Just have someone posted at the entrance to town and we'll pick them up again when they arrive back in Campagna."

"O.K.

Then we're heading home."

*

After a day and night in Sorrento, spending their time basking in the sun and other leisurely pursuits, the couple ferried to the Isle of Capri. Once more, Maria dazzled him with her choice of hotel, the Caesar Augustus. Like the Parco in Sorrento, it too was built on a cliff side, one thousand feet above the water...and had arguably the most spectacular view of Naples and its bay and all points in between as well as the island of Ischia in the distance to the northwest.

"Another five star friend of yours?" he asked as they approached.

"Yes" she answered serenely, leaving the details for him to discover.

And discover they did.

For two full days filled with radiant Tyrrhenian Sea weather, they took in the sites of the island. The intense azure colors emitted by the waters of the world famous Blue Grotto cave left him analyzing the events of the excursion and wondering if it were even possible to name a favorite site or hotel or meal.

From Capri, they boarded a ferry directly to Naples, turned south towards Pompeii, but after a brief discussion elected to drive directly back to Campagna and the business of the Gibboni estate that awaited them.

As they passed back from Eboli to Campagna, they once again were on the radar of the "boss".

"Follow them and see to it that they don't leave town unless someone is on their tail."

*

"Mikey, what are we going to do now?" Agnes had finally settled on this new name for her husband following their reunion in New York.

"We've been out of Italy for some time and no one has bothered us here...so far." Agnes continued to express her concern to him that someone from their past would suddenly appear and change all that in an instant. As far as she was concerned, things had gone all too smoothly up to this point.

"Mama, I've considered that and I've been talking to some people I know from back home. They've told me about a small town in Connecticut where there are jobs available. They're planning on moving there and I think maybe we should join them.

It's called Meriden. There is a big manufacturing company called International Silver. It might be something that the children would be interested in.

And I'd like to open my own barber shop. It would be a good respectable business. I don't think anyone would be looking for me there doing that kind of work. Freddie can join me since he already has training as a barber and eventually he can take over the business. Besides, he can teach me the trade.

I think we should discuss it at dinner one day this week."

"Leave it to me. I'll make my usual Sunday meal and you can bring it up for discussion.

By the way, are you aware that our son has been seeing a young lady from Eboli?

Her name is Maria Salzarulo."

"Yes. He told me about her too.

It's amazing that we lived only eight kilometers apart and now he meets her here in New York. Her family apparently owned a small tomato products company there, but the bad weather over the last decade ruined their business. They came here to find a better life like most of the other Italians we know. I think he is seriously thinking of asking her to marry him.

It's about time he found a wife and started his own family. And if he's lucky, she'll be as good a wife as you have been to me."

He patted her on the rear and then gave her a kiss.

"And if she's the one, perhaps she'll be as lucky as me to have someone that has been as faithful and hopelessly romantic as you."

*

"Mr. Mayor...Antonio...we are back in town, so we'd like to arrange to visit the Gibboni estate at your earliest convenience."

"Maria, if you will allow me to call the appropriate people, I'm sure it can be arranged for later today or tomorrow. Do you have a preference?"

"Since I'm not sure how long we will need to be there... depending on exactly what we find...perhaps tomorrow would be best and the earlier the better too. If it's all right with you, I'm going to bring a friend of mine from Naples who is an expert in old art as well as in genealogy?"

"Of course.

That will be just fine. I will call you back later."

Jack had caught the gist of the conversation but Maria turned and summarized it for him.

"And who is this friend from Naples that you spoke of?"

"His name is Angelo Cassavetes. He was a long time friend of my husbands. I guess I forgot to mention to you that I had talked to him about the portraits immediately after we first saw them. He said he would be more than happy to accompany us when we went to the Gibboni estate.

I need to call and confirm that he will be available to come here in the morning."

While Maria made the call to her friend, he took the time to call back to Georgia and check on things at home. She was pleased to inform him that her friend Angelo would meet them for breakfast at nine the following morning.

He was equally delighted to report to her that all was well at home.

"Oh, I almost forgot" he added.

"I had one of my assistants look up Gibboni on one of the ancestry web sites...and guess what?"

She gave him a blank look.

"My great-grandfather, Michele Catalano, married a woman named Agostina Gibboni. I knew I had heard the name somewhere before from one of my relatives.

So she would be my great-grandmother."

And her father's name was Angelo Gibboni.

So it appears that we have found my great-great-grandfather!"

"That's fantastic!

You may be the only or nearest living relative."

She was interrupted by the ringing of her cell phone.

It was Antonio confirming their excursion to the Gibboni estate the following morning at ten o'clock.

"Well, that's all settled. Now, what would you like to do with the rest of today?" she queried.

"I know how I'd like to start the day...and perhaps finish it as well."

He gave her that unmistakable look, allowing no doubt in her mind as to his meaning.

"You Italian men *are* all alike.

But that's why Italian women stay happy all the time."

She took his hand and led him into the bedroom.

*

On schedule, the following morning precisely at nine o'clock, Maria's friend from Naples arrived at her home in Campagna. She made the necessary introductions and the trio proceeded to the terrace where she had breakfast waiting.

"It's a pleasure to make your acquaintance" Jack said after briefly surveying his physique, secretly delighted to find that Maria's friend Angelo was an elderly Italian gentleman who appeared to be at least sixty-five.

"Would you care for coffee?" Maria queried.

"Espresso, please, if you have it?"

"Yes, of course.

Please help yourself to the food while I get the beverages."

She had laid out a typical European breakfast of meats, cheeses and fruits and fresh rolls that she had purchased at the local bakery a few doors down from her home earlier that morning.

After a few get acquainted remarks, Angelo got right to the point concerning their day's activities.

"Tell me a bit about your family and the association with the Gibbonis."

First he briefed Angelo on the fact that he had recently substantiated that his great-grandmother was a Gibboni and that the owner of the estate was apparently her father and hence his relationship to them.

Then he continued with a summary of the facts that he and Maria had gathered over the preceding several months, including the places they had visited and the various documents they had found that had led them to their pending visit to the Gibboni estate.

"It sounds like you two have done a good deal of homework. I hope that what we see today validates and enhances your findings.

And I hope to be of service in doing just that."

Maria glanced at her kitchen clock.

"My goodness" she exclaimed.

"It's time that we got to the mayor's office. I wouldn't want to be late on this most important day.

It's been a long time coming."

Angelo excused himself and went to the restroom.

"I hope that this day provides the answers that we have been seeking" Maria said, as she took his hand and gave him a brief kiss on the lips.

"As do I" he replied.

Upon Angelo's return from the restroom, the three proceeded to his car and on to the mayor's office.

CHAPTER TWENTY-ONE

"**I** still can't believe that a no name from Georgia has teamed up with this woman and together they may find out the real facts about my family that have remained hidden for so many years.

I swore to never let the truth get out.

The family history needs to stay a secret.

I know I haven't exactly given it a good name lately, but still no one knows the real truth except for a few close friends…including you two."

Toto was speaking by phone from America to the pair that had been his closest associates in Italy for decades. He had left them in charge of his affairs at home when he found it necessary to escape to New York.

"Boss, our lookout near her home just called and said they're back in town, so we'd better get going.

We'll call you as soon as we know something. You can tell us how you want it handled then."

"O.K. But I may well have to come there and get involved in this one myself."

*

The trio walked into the mayor's office.

"It's good to see you both" Antonio said. He gave Maria a warm hug.

"And this must be the friend from Naples that you spoke so highly of?"

She turned and introduced Angelo Cassavetes to him.

Antonio gave the older gentleman a hearty handshake and welcomed him to Campagna.

"Have you been to our fair city before?"

"No. I've been to Eboli but only because it is on the main highway. Despite my previous dealings with this lovely lady's late husband, we were generally in Naples or Florence or at an exhibition site in numerous larger cities around the country.

But, today it is my pleasure to be here. I only hope that my presence can be helpful to my friends" he added, gesturing towards the couple who were seated on the only divan in the office.

Antonio turned back towards the couple.

"And how was your trip to Amalfi?"

She gave him a brief synopsis of the attractions that they had visited.

Antonio glanced at his watch.

"Well, I think that we should be going. I told Gina…the person that is showing us the estate…that we would be there by ten-thirty. It's only about a fifteen minute drive so we should be just on time."

*

A small route exited the city towards the north into the hills above Campagna. These were some of the smaller peaks of the Apennines but majestic in their relationship to the plains below. At the summit of one of these was the Gibboni estate. As they approached, the occupants of the vehicle were all struck by the size of it. The property was surrounded by an impressive wrought iron fence that resembled Roman spears held in position by horizontal bars. A large gate, remotely operated, marked the entrance.

Without delay, the grand gate opened and allowed them entrance at the sound of the mayor's voice.

The driveway to the main house was at least a half mile long and followed a serpentine course. It was lined with Italian cypress trees that, judging from their size, Angelo estimated at over fifty years of age.

"This variety of tree is generally slow growing. To reach a height in excess of twenty-five feet and to have a base as broad as those, they would have to be at least that old."

The lined portion of driveway soon segued into a clearing that ended with a circular portion that led to the home's main entrance and a smaller road that led from the circle to the garage area. There were at least six doors that they could see from their vantage point, but the road appeared to continue around a curve toward the back of the house.

As they stepped from the car, the magnificent twin front doors opened and a figure appeared.

"Antonio, it's good to see you again" said the fairly attractive woman that Maria estimated to be in her mid-forties.

"Gina, these are my friends."

Antonio introduced each by name.

"And this is Gina Cerasale, the executor of the estate."

"Are you related to the Gibboni family?" Maria asked.

"I was married to one of Angelo Gibboni's nephews. Unfortunately, my husband died in an accident several years ago."

"Then, we may be distantly related by marriage" Jack added.

"My great-grandmother was Agostina Gibboni. She married my great-grandfather, Michele Catalano. Agostina's father was an Angelo too. So the owner of this estate must have been a great grandson or grandnephew."

"I will have to consult the family genealogy charts" Gina responded.

I don't recall the name, but it is quite possible that it is there.

There are no living children and there were no grandchildren... so up to now, that just leaves me...and now you.

I have spent a fair amount of time here since Mr. Gibboni died, but as you can see the estate is rather enormous and I'm sure there are many parts of it that even I haven't seen.

So, if you are ready, we can begin.

Or if you would prefer, we can have espresso in the kitchen and I can show you some papers that demonstrate the layout of the estate. I can then give you a quick tour before beginning a detailed examination."

They mutually decided that the latter suggestion would be most helpful in deciding how best to approach seeing all areas of the estate. With the drawings, they could make sure that they didn't miss an area, which they all concurred would be easy to do without a plan and a way to note the areas that had been seen from those still left to be investigated.

Following espresso, during which time they examined the plans, and following a bathroom break, they set out on the expedited tour.

"If you will follow me", said Gina.

*

What little of the morning remained disappeared quickly as they were given the cursory look at the villa. The group decided it prudent to stop for lunch at one p.m. before proceeding to the more detailed examination of the estate. This would begin with the more mundane portions of the estate initially, including the kitchen, dining room and bedrooms in the main house. Once these areas were inspected, they would proceed to the larger rooms generally reserved for entertaining party guests, toward the rear of the main floor.

Then would follow several attached add-on portions including a vast game room that would need their scrutiny, before proceeding to the unattached areas that included several small guest villas, a pool house with attached bath house and the garages and stables.

The estate still retained a staff to care for day to day needs of the home and grounds including a chef to prepare meals for the caretaker staff and visitors. By the time they had returned to the main dining area, a sumptuous luncheon was awaiting them.

Maria turned and said quietly: "Even I don't think I can eat a large meal like this. It's only been a few hours since breakfast." He whispered his concurrence.

"Back home in Georgia, we usually just have a sandwich, a bag of chips and a Coke for lunch. Our big meal is in the evening."

"I hope everyone is hungry" said their hostess, Gina.

"Franco has prepared one of his very special pasta dishes for us" she said referring to her chef who stood smiling at the group from the head of the table.

"Mange".

The couple smiled at each other. They sat down and did their best to enjoy the meal, not wanting to offend their hostess or the chef. By the time they finished, each felt totally sated and ready for a siesta...common in many European countries during mid-afternoon.

"I'm not used to drinking wine with every meal like you do in your country" he whispered to Maria.

"Frankly, it makes me very tired."

But there was much work to be done.

*

The detailed investigation was proceeding according to plan with nothing of interest being found in the main living areas. Gina having already gathered her maps and notes was bounding off towards the next area on their itinerary. The grand ball room at the rear of the main house was an extraordinary sized room with lavish ceiling and three large crystal chandeliers that separated the floor into three sections. The wall facing the rear of the estate was essentially one large glass pane separated and supported by narrow bands of steel. The view of the property containing a small lake and floral gardens well beyond the pool and pool house was equally spectacular. On the interior wall there were several large portraits of Antonio Gibboni and his wife, Eleanora, and other members of their family including their daughter, Lucia. Each was labeled as to the subject, the date of the painting and the artist.

*

They quickly dispatched the pool and pool house. While the Olympic size structure was unique in its design and location, it held little of interest regarding their mission at the estate.

The stables too were interesting and remarkably clean and well kept despite the absence of any horses, gone since the demise of Antonio. And the garages were equally large and well maintained. They contained a small collection of antique Italian autos including a Bugatti and several classic Ferraris.

The men were thrilled to be in the presence of such automobile royalty and would have liked to linger a bit; but the women showed no enthusiasm for the cars and so they quickly moved on.

"I think we should go back to the main house. I believe there is some sort of basement that purportedly can be reached from the master bedroom. I've never actually looked for the stairwell, but I'm told there is supposed to be one" Gina suggested.

Maria confided to her that they had reviewed the plans from the estate and didn't recall any mention of it.

"Well, I guess there's one way to find out.

Let's go check it out.

With five of us, if something's there, we're bound to find it."

*

The master bedroom was larger than any of the grand suites they had occupied during their visit to the Amalfi Coast and Capri.

It not only contained a king size bed with canopy, large end tables with tall lamps adjacent to each side, and a wooden chest at the foot, but also a large sitting area facing a hearth replete with love seat and several recliner chairs. A large flat screen television was mounted above the mantle.

Twin bathrooms led from the bedroom toward one side and matching twin walk-in closets opposed them.

The members of the party spread out and agreed not to leave an inch of the generous space untouched. Angelo, who up to this point had said little, remarked that the plans suggested space within the closet that didn't seem to match what they were observing.

Antonio, apart from being mayor of the small town of Campagna, owned and operated a construction company as well.

He inspected the plans and made notation of the fact that behind some shelving there would appear to be room for a stairwell…if they could figure out just how an opening could have been fashioned.

"Angelo, you're quite correct. I'm not sure how we didn't see it when we inspected the plans the first time."

After investing almost half an hour inspecting the area from every conceivable angle, they were ready to give up their search and look for other possibilities when Maria took the liberty to remove a few large boxes from a rack above a row of hangars adjacent to the shelves. The hangars held what appeared to be a set of heavy curtains.

She turned to Angelo who was observing her every move and asked him to lift the hangers off the rack.

As he did, a creaking noise suddenly began from a point somewhere below the shelves and within a minute or two the entire shelf elevated itself from the flooring and turned perpendicular to the floor, both blocking the entrance to the closet from the bedroom and also revealing a stairwell leading downward, presumably into the basement they sought.

They all stood within the closet and watched as the astonishing event unfolded.

"Well, I don't know what we did" Jack said to Maria, "but whatever it was we seem to have found the secret we were looking for.

Who's up for a little adventure?" he queried the group.

"It's what we came for" said Antonio. He was quickly seconded by the others.

"Now, if there is just a light switch here." After a few minutes of looking and feeling for one on the dark stairway walls, the group concluded that flashlights would be necessary.

Gina stood in awe of the discovery, claiming no prior knowledge of the passageway that they had found. She was quick to provide them all the lighting they would need from a satchel she had stored in the bedroom.

"We always keep a large supply of flashlights and batteries in case of storms and loss of electricity. It's a big dark place out here in the mountains when the power goes out."

With flashlights in hand, the group proceeded slowly down the steps in search of what they did not know, but could only hope were answers to the questions they had regarding the Gibbonis and the Catalanos, the relationships between the two families, and the identity of the figures in the paintings at the museum and the church.

CHAPTER TWENTY-TWO

After advancing only a few steps into the black void, aided by the flashlights Gina had provided, Angelo was able to locate a set of switches along one wall.

"There.

That's better."

A series of fluorescent light boxes illuminated the darkness that only a moment before portended evil and the unknown. Now with the light emanating from the row of metallic fixtures, they could clearly see that the basement had a central hallway and what appeared to be a series of rooms or additional passageways leading from it.

A lingering residue of mildew floated in the air.

"I wonder just how long it has been since anyone was down here?" queried Maria.

"Judging from the dust on everything and the odor, I'd say it's been quite a while."

Gina, who had maintained her place at the tail end of the search party, looked on in utter amazement.

"All this time I have been here and all I knew was that there was some kind of basement, but I always envisioned a small space for storage. I never would have imagined a long hallway and so many rooms.

How could no one mention that this was all here?" she shouted excitedly.

"Someone must have had a good reason to want to hide it. And I guess our job is to find out just what that reason was" added Angelo.

"Perhaps we should begin?" indicating his curiosity level was rising. He surveyed the faces of the others and they nodded their heads in agreement.

He took the lead, with the others following immediately behind, huddled together like a small herd of sheep fearing a predator attack at any moment.

After tiptoeing about twenty steps, immediately to their right they approached a heavy wooden door with a large iron deadbolt on the outside. The rust on the exterior of the bolt suggested it had not been opened for an extended period of time and that disengaging it might be difficult.

Angelo lifted the bolt and was pleasantly surprised to find that it rotated easily and pulled back with little effort, allowing the door to be pushed inward revealing a cubicle he estimated to be about ten feet square.

"Let me see one of the larger flashlights" he said to Gina.

"Look", he exclaimed as he gazed into the now partially lit room.

"More paintings...and they look very similar to the ones at the museum and at the church."

He continued to search the room for another light source, finally locating a switch behind the door.

The room was immediately flooded with light, illuminating a series of paintings that covered the four walls.

"My God" he uttered. "I think we've hit the jackpot."

Maria turned to Jack: "They must all be relatives of yours.

Just like the ones in town, you resemble them."

Once again he was stunned at the finding. He stood and studied the faces on the portraits before him. On the middle of the bottom portion of the frame was a small metal nameplate, rusting and covered with dust.

Angelo reached into his coat pocket and produced a cloth he had brought with him for just these purposes.

"Here. Use this to clean it."

With a little effort, the letters inscribed on the nameplate became legible.

"Il Padrino...Michele Catalano."

"Then these must be portraits of the same person made at different times."

"No, I hardly think so" volunteered Angelo.

"Look at the clothing" he bade the others.

"I think these are relatives of one another, but the clothing types suggest different time periods."

The others surveyed the paintings in the room and nodded in agreement with Angelo's observation.

"I think we had better see what other surprises this place holds before we render any judgments about the subjects in these portraits...or just what the whole mystery portends.

Let me lead the way."

*

"I feel like we're in the catacombs" Maria exclaimed.

"I still can't believe that all of this was right here under my nose all this time", repeated Gina.

The main hallway continued far beyond the boundaries of the main house and took a series of twists and turns that no one would have predicted from the entrance point below the closet or with their initial view of the hallway from that point.

In addition to a series of separate rooms immediately off the hallway, they were surprised to find a large chamber at the very end of the main corridor that resembled a more modern set of living quarters complete with a rustic kitchen and bathroom facilities. A gravity driven water conduit that appeared to come from somewhere outside the facility flowed into a marble receptacle; an attached drain pipe to keep it from overflowing disappeared into the floor.

"I'm guessing" Angelo interjected, "that much like an underground cave, the temperature remains fairly constant.

And there's even some type of fan mechanism over here."

He pointed to a series of fans mounted on a belt that could be turned with a small hand crank situated on the side.

"It's obvious that electricity wasn't here when this place was constructed.

Look," he said, pointing to oily residue on the walls and ceilings.

"The fan must have helped dissipate the smoke. There must be an outlet somewhere or they would have died from carbon monoxide accumulation.

Does anyone have a match?"

Puzzled at the request, Antonio reached into his jacket pocket and produced a small box of wooden matches and handed it to Angelo.

They stepped into a doorway. Angelo took a match from the box and struck it.

"See, the fumes are moving in that direction" he said, pointing toward one of the rooms near the end of the hallway.

"There must be an exhaust mechanism there.

It was all very well planned, as if someone were going to stay down here for an extended period of time."

"So, what does it all mean?"

Angelo, the research specialist and antiquarian of the group, offered little in the way of explanation.

"Frankly, I don't know.

I expect it's going to take some time to unravel the whole mystery. I think we need to take one room at a time and see what names we can find on the portraits. That and any other clues that we find might allow us to make some type of educated guess.

One thing that I think we can conclude for sure: the histories of the Catalano family and Angelo Gibboni are interwoven and we need to find out just how!"

*

"Boss", he whispered into his cell phone, "they must have found the secret hideout."

"How can you be sure?" came the gruff reply from Toto. He used a speakerphone situated next to the Jacuzzi in which he relaxed while sipping a glass of Chianti and smoking a Cuban cigar.

"Well, I can see some smoke coming from the small pipes that were installed to allow exhaust when the fans were in use. And, just to be sure, I've checked the electricity meter we had installed for that part of the house only. It's showing power is in use as we speak."

"Damn. I was stupidly hoping no one would ever stumble onto it. Now the family history will be made public again. It's amazing how stories can die out after a few generations …if you let them… and how quickly they can be resurrected when you least expect it.

I guess it's time for me to pay a visit to my old home once more. I'll let you know when my plane will be arriving into Naples and you can pick me up there.

Good job."

"Thanks, Boss.

I'll be expecting your call."

*

Angelo was a good organizer and it was immediately obvious to the entire group that he was knowledgeable about a full range of subjects concerning antiquities.

"We're going to have to go through each room and take photos of each of the portraits. Hopefully, each one has a nameplate or something on the back that will help in the identification of the subject.

Once we have all the pictures, we can enlarge them digitally and try to make comparisons…that is, try to determine if we are looking at the same person at a different time in his life or entirely separate figures.

We can also use the clothing they are wearing to try to estimate the exact time period if there are no dates on the portraits to help us. And if all else fails, we can take samples from the painting themselves and attempt carbon dating of the paint materials.

If we can get permission, I think the first thing we need to do is enlarge the entrance from the closet where we found the secret passage. It's going to be tough to keep going in and out through such a small opening and virtually impossible to bring any equipment down here that we might need."

He glanced at Mayor Badalementi.

Antonio understood his role in that.

"I'll see to it right away" he pledged to Angelo.

"I think perhaps it would be best if we wait for additional permission before we continue. And I think it is understood that no one in this room need say a word about our findings to anyone else."

He turned to each one in turn and received an affirmation.

"Then let's call it a day.

Perhaps an aperitif is in order?"

They left and drove back to town after placing objects in the closet back as they had been before their discovery.

CHAPTER TWENTY-THREE

Antonio had no problem convincing the Campagna city council members to approve enlargement of the entrance into the newly discovered basement area with the one caveat that things would have to be restored to their original state unless determined otherwise at the completion of their mission. The council members had been appointed as co-executors of the Gibboni estate pending the identification and authentication of the closest remaining living descendent(s).

All agreed to the terms.

It remained then for the mayor, assisted by Angelo, to engage a construction company to do the necessary work. Since dealing with old dwellings was an everyday occurrence in the small ancient town as well as the surrounding area, he quickly signed a contract with Arturo Tosca and Co., a local firm that he knew well and trusted. They enjoyed an excellent reputation in the town as well as in the entire Campania region.

Arturo informed the mayor that it would be necessary to fully inspect the home and basement in order to prepare an estimate of cost and to determine precisely what equipment and supplies would be needed for the job.

The following morning Arturo and his oldest son Mario visited the home in the company of Antonio and Angelo.

"Antonio, I should be able to have an estimate for you by late this afternoon, and I'm sure we can begin the work within two days. We already have most of the equipment that we will need right here in town and I'm sure I can arrange to get the few remaining items from a source I have in Eboli."

"Then it is agreed. I will wait for your call with the estimate."

The mayor and Angelo returned to town to relay the events of the morning to the remaining members of the group; Antonio indicated that he would let them know when construction would begin as soon as he heard from Arturo and contracts were signed. Everyone agreed that they would want to be present...both to help where they could, but mostly to be on hand should anything important be discovered...beyond what they had already seen.

*

"How was your flight, Boss?"

Ralph was waiting by the carousel in the baggage claim area when Toto appeared on the escalator that conveyed him from the arrival floor to the lower level.

"Long and bumpy!" was his curt reply.

"Damn flight was an hour late getting out of Kennedy because of thunderstorms in the area. That's the trouble with flights that leave late afternoon or early evening, especially from Long Island."

He had been on the Delta non-stop from JFK to Rome and after a short layover had taken an Alitalia flight from Rome to Naples.

"The weather coming into Rome was a bit testy as well...some light rain and crosswinds. I thought the plane was going to be blown off the runway for a minute as we were landing.

We had to abort the landing, take off and land again from a different direction."

Ralph wasn't used to the boss chattering on like this. Usually he barely said hello and traveled in relative silence unless he wanted to stop for a bathroom break or get a cup of coffee or occasionally smoke a cigar.

Toto had a rule about smoking in the car: *no one smoked in the car*! Not even him. While he liked the taste and smell of cigars as they were being consumed, he did not like the stale odor they left behind in confined spaces such as a car.

"Do you have luggage?"

Ralph asked the boss what seemed to him a simple and harmless question.

Toto turned and stared directly at him.

"No, dummy" was his sarcastic reply.

"Ralph, do you really think I came all this way with only the clothes on my back and nothing to shave or brush my teeth with?"

Ralph awkwardly replied.

"Sorry, Boss.

Of course you have luggage. What does it look like?"

"It just so happens that it is coming down the conveyor right now" he said, pointing to a tan leather bag with the large initials "TC" on the side.

"Smart.

Very smart" uttered Ralph.

He grabbed the bag and led the way to the passport control where he was quickly cleared.

"Luigi is waiting in the car. I'll call him on my cell phone and he'll be here in a minute or two."

Toto glanced at him with another disapproving look, indicating his distaste at waiting even a minute for anyone.

Luigi appeared instantly, appeasing Toto to some extent.

"Nice wheels" he said.

He was ushered into the Mercedes 600 sedan. Immediately, Luigi accelerated out of the airport confines en route to the autostrada that would take them towards their destination.

"I have a bottle of your favorite scotch and some ice and glasses in the bar."

"That's very thoughtful, Luigi."

Ralph motioned towards Toto.

"One or two fingers?"

"Three! And a single ice cube."

"I thought you'd like to get some rest today after your overnight flight. We can proceed to the Campagna area tomorrow. They've just started working on the basement access in the past few days."

"That will be fine" Toto responded.

The scotch was already hitting its mark…Toto was mellowing out and agreeing with his employees.

Ralph and Luigi accepted that as a good sign.

"We'll stop in Battipaglia if that's o.k. with you?"

Ralph glanced at Toto and reached over and took the glass of scotch from his hand. He was already asleep.

"I'll take that as a sign that it's o.k." Ralph relayed to Luigi.

*

On the morning of the first day of the project at the Gibboni estate, Arturo Tosca had sent his son Mario to begin the job. Mario had been working as an apprentice to his father for several years, but some projects still needed the input from someone with much more experience than he had accumulated in that short time.

Arturo arrived about two hours later. Mario briefed him on what he had found with his initial excavation and after a short inspection of the problem, Arturo quickly agreed that he had underestimated things.

Angelo, who had accompanied the pair, could easily appreciate the problem that they had encountered.

"The entrance has been constructed almost like a bomb shelter. It's much thicker brick and concrete than I anticipated. The way the bricks have been laid and secured together is like something you might expect to see in diggings in Egypt or ancient Rome.

In addition, the mechanism that moves the shelving to expose the stairwell is a system of weights and pulleys and rotating drums. So it's going to require some ingenuity to figure this all out and… I'm not sure I can guarantee getting it back to its original state as we promised the city counsel in return for allowing us to excavate the site."

"I see your dilemma" said Angelo.

"If I may suggest" he said, looking at Arturo.

"I have an acquaintance in Naples who has worked at the Pompeii and Herculaneum dig sites. I think he might be just the person to help us with this problem…if he's available."

"Contact him" Arturo responded without hesitation.

Angelo returned to the main part of the house where his cell phone would receive a signal and placed the call.

Fortunately, his friend was home and not engaged at the moment. He would be available to come to Campagna that same afternoon.

*

Angelo watched as the small Lamborghini sports car negotiated the final turns up the long entranceway into the Gibboni estate. The rather handsome young man dressed in slacks, pastel shirt and matching blazer with flaming red handkerchief emblazoning the pocket emerged from the vehicle and walked toward Angelo.

"Ciao" they said heartily to one another followed by a series of hugs and pats on the back.

Angelo turned toward the group now assembled to greet the person they hoped could solve their predicament.

"My friends, this is my colleague for many years, Dr. Eugenio Roncalli. He's really not as young as he looks…he just inherited better genes than I did."

The group laughed in response.

Angelo then introduced each of the members of the group by name.

When he came to Maria, he hesitated for a moment.

Eugenio extended his hand gently toward hers, lifted it and kissed it gracefully.

"I didn't know there would be a famous movie star here. I never thought that I would have the opportunity to meet you, Ms. Loren.

And please call me Gene…everyone else does."

Angelo delayed any response, allowing his friends to revel in the moment.

Everyone smiled as they waited for Maria to respond

"Thank you for your kind words…but I'm afraid that I only look like Sophia Loren.

My real name is Maria Rosato. And this is my fiancé.

I hope I haven't disappointed you too much."

Gene laughed.

"Well, whoever you are, it's a pleasure to meet you.

And you, sir, are a lucky man to have such a beautiful bride to be."

"Thank you. I am already aware of that.

And may I ask just what type of doctor you are? By the way, nice car."

"I have a Ph.D. in archeology…I'm one of those people you see on T.V. and in movies who runs around the world digging up old buildings and old bones."

"Sort of like Indiana Jones?" Maria added.

He laughed.

"Sort of.

But not as handsome as Harrison Ford."

Maria thought silently that he underestimated himself...that he was far more handsome than the movie star. But she felt it best to keep that thought to herself, given the fact that she was standing next to her fiance and in the company of a whole group of people that might misinterpret such a comment.

Gene turned back to Jack. "And thank you. I just acquired the car. It's a lot of fun to drive."

When the introductions were done and some small talk concluded, Angelo escorted his guest inside the house to inspect the problem area. After an hour or more of scrutiny around the stairwell entrance, Gene announced his verdict.

"You really do have a problem.

I've researched a few similar buildings and it won't be easy...but I think I can show you how to disassemble things...and put them back together much as you found them."

CHAPTER TWENTY-FOUR

Arturo, accompanied by his son Mario, and Gene Roncalli together compiled a list of all the additional equipment they would need for the dismantling phase of the project. By the following morning, the wheels were well in motion to have everything necessary on site in the shortest possible time. Gene's connections in Naples as well as several other nearby towns were instrumental in assuring the availability of the gear.

By early on the second day following Gene's arrival, the project was well under way and access to the basement had been enhanced considerably.

"As soon as we can disengage the belts that permit the drums to turn in unison, we can lift them from the basement. Then we can shore up the remaining shaft on all four sides. That should allow us ample space to come and go as we please with the addition of some steps.

We also have a lift mechanism that we can send to the basement level and back to retrieve the objects you've found so that we can inspect them in better light.

By the way, how do you plan to proceed with the items once they're removed from the basement?" Gene asked Angelo.

"We haven't fully discussed it yet among the group, but I think we need to remove everything to somewhere here in the house or one of the adjacent buildings, inventory them and then decide exactly what will need to be done to identify and restore them if necessary. Since it appears that all these paintings and other objects have been here for quite a while, I'm sure a lot of work will need to be done. The portraits will surely need to be cleaned to better assist in identifying the subject of the painting and perhaps the artist if they are not signed.

Needless to say, that could require quite a bit of time and money."

"Well, Angelo my friend, things seem to be progressing well here and I'm afraid I'll need to get back to Naples by early afternoon since I have a flight to Cairo in the morning. But I'll be back in a week and will call you to see how things are progressing. I'll make sure that I'm available to help you in the restoration phase."

"You will stay for lunch?

The others would like to hear what you have to say and we can discuss how we're going to handle things once they've been extricated from the basement."

"Of course.

I wouldn't want to miss seeing your lovely Sophia Loren look-alike one more time before I go."

"Be careful.

I don't think her fiancé would appreciate a rival with your good looks. Of course, they don't know about your reputation as I do."

"You flatter me, Angelo."

"Only because I am jealous of someone your age...and your reputation!"

*

Gina's kitchen staff had been busy preparing lunch all morning while the others had concerned themselves with the basement issue. Promptly at twelve-thirty, she announced it time to come to the dining room on the terrace where all was in readiness.

After the blessing had been said, they all engaged in conversation as the antipasti were served and the wine poured. Over an entrée of chicken Marsala and side dishes of Tuscan potatoes and meat stuffed bell peppers, Angelo initiated a discussion on how to handle the artifacts as they were brought up from the basement. Since he was the authority, everyone deferred to his expertise.

Gina's chef followed with a pasta dish of linguine smothered with tomato sauce and Italian sausage.

Lambrusco wine from a vintner in the hills above Campagna flowed freely as she completed the feast with individual servings of tiramisu.

"I hope that I can get back to Naples without falling asleep" Gene commented as he rose to leave.

"My thanks to all of you for your hospitality.

I will be in touch next week" he said to Angelo as he strode to his car.

Then he revved the Lamborghini engine for all to hear and departed in a cloud of dust down the long driveway.

"My, he certainly is a showoff" Jack whispered to Maria.

She smiled demurely at her fiancé and held his hand in silence as they watched the Lamborghini disappear from sight.

*

Gene Roncalli had barely made it half way from Campagna to Eboli when he suddenly realized that someone had pulled out behind him just after he had rounded one of the many curves on the mountainous road between the two towns. The small sedan had continued to tail him at a safe distance of about a quarter of a mile ever since.

He attempted to convince himself that it was just a coincidence since the road was narrow and windy, and opportunities to pass were few. But when he reached one of the straight stretches and slowed down to let the vehicle pass, it maintained the same relative position.

"Perhaps they're just not in a hurry" he contemplated to himself.

He was nearing one of the narrowest parts of the highway just before the approach into Eboli when he spotted something blocking the road a few hundred feet ahead. Proceeding slowly, he stopped when he saw that a vehicle was in the middle of the road with its hood raised, and that there was no way around the obstruction it caused.

What appeared to be a single male person stood looking under the raised hood of a van. Gene could see steam rising from the engine block.

Assuming that he might be of help since he kept a spare water container in his trunk, he exited his car and approached the man.

Before he could say a word, another figure hidden from sight on the opposite side of the vehicle leapt in his direction and threw a cloth over his face. The one who had been standing in front of the car then grabbed his hands and wrenched them behind his back and applied a pair of cuffs. The pair quickly wrestled him into the back seat of the stalled vehicle and held a rag under his nose.

And then all went blank.

*

Gene's next recollection was awakening in an unfamiliar room with a terrible headache. He was tied to a chair in a most uncomfortable position. His mouth felt like someone had stuffed cotton balls into it and he had to struggle to take a breath.

After a few agonizing minutes that felt like hours, a door to the room opened and two men entered...presumably the same two that had abducted him. They were soon joined by a third man who spoke both Italian and English, and who apparently was the one in charge.

All wore masks over their faces...presumably so that they could not be recognized by their captive. One walked to his side and stood silently.

"Just what are you and your friends doing in the basement of the Gibboni estate?"

He related to the man how he had been asked by his friend Angelo Cassavetes to help in the excavation project at the home.

"Then you had no prior knowledge of the estate or its contents... or of Angelo Gibboni?"

"None.

It is just as I have told you" he repeated.

"I just came at the request of an old friend who needed my kind of help."

"We shall see. We shall see" the man answered.

Then once again a hand came from behind...and all went dark.

*

When Gene awoke, his head was about to explode once again. His vision slowly cleared as he surveyed his surroundings. It appeared that he was now in a different room without any windows and only a single door. As soon as he felt enough strength return in his legs, and discovering that he was not restrained in any way, he stood and approached the door. It was locked as he assumed it would be. He tried turning the knob with both hands, pulling on it with one foot against the wall, but to no avail.

At least he wasn't in the dark and the room temperature was comfortable.

He suddenly remembered the cell phone that he carried in the inside pocket of his sport coat, but a quick check proved that it had been removed. As he glanced around he saw that there was a cot in addition to the chair that he had been seated in when he awoke. For the moment, he was content to lie on the cot and try to organize his thoughts and let the headache pass.

*

Back at the Gibboni estate the following day, things were progressing, albeit slowly. Angelo proceeded with inspection of several of the portraits as the equipment ordered by Gene Roncalli slowly arrived.

Gina approached Angelo with a portable phone in her hand.

"It's for you" she said.

"Pronto!" he spoke into the phone.

Gina and the others watched his facial contortions as he listened to the caller. After several minutes, he thanked the caller and hung up.

"That was a friend of Gene Roncalli. Gene had told him where he was going. He got concerned this morning when Gene didn't make his flight to Cairo. He has been unable to contact him either directly at his home or on his cell phone.

It seems that we apparently were the last ones to have seen him before his disappearance!"

CHAPTER TWENTY-FIVE

They decided to follow the route that they presumed Gene would have taken to Naples in hopes of gleaning some useful information concerning his disappearance. Given the events unfolding over the past several days, they assumed them to be related somehow.

Neither he nor Maria were big believers in coincidence.

They all agreed not to involve the police right away since it had only been a matter of hours that Gene was presumed to be missing.

Angelo and the others were hard at work at the Gibboni estate now that all the special equipment was in place.

By mid-morning, they were in her Fiat bound for Eboli with plans to continue on to Naples if necessary. They weren't sure why, but they had high expectations that they could resolve the mystery of Gene's vanishing before the end of the day, and then return to the Gibboni estate while it was still light enough to see the progress made at the excavation site during their absence.

Just on the outskirts of Eboli, Jack yelled out:

"Stop the car.

Look over there along the side the road."

The brakes screeched as she followed his command and turned the Fiat toward the shoulder of the road.

He got out and walked the few feet to where the object lay.

Picking it up, he held it where she could see it from her position on the driver's side of the car.

"Why, isn't that....?"

"Exactly!

It's the handkerchief that Gene wore in his coat pocket. I couldn't help but notice the brilliant color...and the amazing contrast with his sports coat."

He surveyed the area around where the scarf had been.

"There are a lot of foot marks here, like someone had been scuffling."

By now, Maria had exited the car so that she could see firsthand the things he was pointing at.

"It looks like at least three sets of foot prints here...and then only two where they disappear back onto the pavement."

"They must have carried him off" she said.

He turned to look at her with a grin on his face.

"My, my...aren't we turning into the amateur detectives?

But now, I think we are obligated to notify the Italian authorities. It looks like someone has probably kidnapped him."

"But why?" she queried.

"I don't know, but once again I don't believe in coincidences. It's got to be related to what we're doing. And don't forget the people that have been following us at various times over the past month or so.

Everything must have a connection...and we've got to figure out how to connect the dots."

There was that look on her face again.

He explained "connecting dots."

Then she turned back toward the Fiat, wearing a profoundly worried look on her face.

*

"Boss, I think this guy is telling the truth.

I think he just came to help them at the estate like he said. I don't think he knows anything about the family history."

"Perhaps you're right.

In fact, I agree with you.

Did he get a look at either of your faces when you put him into the van?"

"I don't think he could have...in fact, I'm sure he didn't. We had our faces covered just like you told us."

"And I came up behind him and held the chloroform over his mouth and nose until he was unconscious."

"Then take him and his car back to where you found him and let him go."

The two looked at each other in amazement, perplexed by the boss's uncharacteristic kindness.

Usually the boss gave orders for an execution unflinchingly and left them with the task of figuring out the method of implementing his command, followed by disposing of the body where it hopefully wouldn't be found.

"Yes sir," was all they could say.

*

Gene heard the door being opened...and once again was unconscious before he could comprehend what was happening. His next recollection was awakening in his car on the road between Campagna and Eboli...with a splitting headache once again.

But...he realized that he was still alive and apparently free, something he couldn't have envisioned only a few hours earlier while being interrogated by his trio of captors.

*

Jack and Maria had just left the Eboli Polizia station, after providing them with all the information they knew about Eugene Roncalli and his sudden and mysterious disappearance.

They had had little time to be alone since the events unfolding at the Gibboni estate had taken precedence in their lives, so they decided to stop for lunch at Pasquales, the restaurant in Eboli where they had dined on the day they first met.

"You know", he said "we were talking about marriage plans until all this family business sort of got in the way."

Maria held his hand tighter.

"My darling, I know you love me and just as soon as we get this whole thing resolved, we can go ahead with those plans.

But I know how important this family business is to you...and now to me as well.

It's more imperative than ever that we find out what's happened to Gene Roncalli and see things to a conclusion at the Gibboni estate as well.

And...I've got to know just who has been following us and why!"

He looked at her with uncustomary compassion in his eyes.

"God, I really love you" was all he could say.

She smiled.

After a few moments of lingering silence between them, she excused herself and went to the ladies room while lunch was being prepared.

*

"I'm told that some Mafia boss from the U.S. may be here in Campania.

Find out who it is and where he is if you can and get back to me as soon as possible" she whispered into her cell phone, taking precautions that no one could hear her conversation.

Then she returned to the table where the food was waiting.

"Now, let's eat. It all looks so delicious.

Then we need to get back to the estate and see what new and interesting facts Angelo has for us."

*

About five minutes out of Eboli en route to Campagna, Maria noticed a vehicle stalled on the side of the road. She slowed down and approached it cautiously.

"It's a Lamborghini, and it looks just like Gene's.

I can't see anyone in it, can you?"

He nodded 'no'.

The pair quickly exited the Fiat and walked guardedly toward the car.

There on the front seat lay Gene Roncalli, holding his head.

He turned toward the pair, sat up and said in a quasi-mocking tone:

"Well, it's about time!"

They laughed in response to his humor and she hugged him as they did.

A brief conversation told the couple that he was not clear enough mentally to tell them what had happened and how he'd come to be back on the road where only hours earlier they'd deduced that he had been abducted.

"Now, let's get back to the estate.

I'll take your car.

You go with Maria in the Fiat since I don't think you're in any condition to be driving right now."

"I'll have to concur with that" Gene answered.

Once en route to Campagna, Gene turned to Maria.

"I'll tell you what little I can when we get back to the estate. Meanwhile, do you have any thing for a headache?"

She smiled.

"Yes, I believe I do if you will hand me my purse. You look as though you could use an aspirin or two."

*

"Even though I don't feel any bruises on my head, I feel like someone hit me with a large bat."

"Being drugged will do that to you. By the way, I notified the Polizia in Eboli that we brought you here. They're going to send someone later today to talk to you."

"I don't know if I can be of much help."

"Perhaps your memory will improve after that headache goes away" added Maria.

"Why don't you get a little rest while we check on Angelo's progress? Is there anyone that we should notify that you're safe and sound?"

"Just the person that you said called to report that I had missed my flight. I think I remember his phone number.

And Sophia...I'm sorry, Maria...thank you both for your kindness."

Once again, she could only smile.

*

The excavation was proceeding slowly, but steadily.

The equipment that Gene had helped procure had arrived and allowed Angelo and his crew to enlarge the opening and construct a temporary staircase to the basement of the estate. The lift was positioned near the opening and facilitated bringing heavy items to the main level with ease.

They also enlarged one of the doors to the patio to make removal of the art work and other items from the house easier. On the patio itself, a large tent had been raised to protect the recovered treasures from the elements until they could be transported the short distance to the multi-car garage that now was being transformed into the repository for the artifacts...and the site where Angelo had chosen to do preliminary work on identification and cataloguing.

Jack and Maria talked briefly to Angelo, who despite his age, looked like a schoolboy on his first date. His enthusiasm for the project was infectious. His crew went about their work with uncustomary passion and care.

"We're used to working on ancient and religious sites" he said to the couple.

"So to us, this is almost the same. After all, it is sacred to someone...and since you may be the only true family member we know of at this time, it should be especially to you."

Jack said nothing for a moment or two.

"You know, I never thought of it that way, but you are right.

We are in the process of unlocking the past that undoubtedly contains several centuries of the history of my relatives. And if the research that Maria and I have done is borne out by these findings...it will connect me to some of the most fascinating and well known people of Italian and Spanish antiquity.

Thank you for that thought, Angelo."

He just smiled contentedly.

"Now, my friends, let me get back to work."

*

The next several days passed by uneventfully as more portraits were removed from the basement to the patio and ultimately to the garage repository.

Gene Roncalli had been visited by the Polizia several times. On the most recent interview, he had suddenly remembered a fact that had escaped him on their initial encounter.

"I seem to remember the one in charge...the one the others called 'Boss'...didn't have a European accent at all. The other two were definitely Italian, but 'Boss' spoke with an American accent... possibly from the New York area."

The Polizia seemed energized by that piece of news. Apparently, as they had shared with the couple earlier, there had been reports of a big time crime boss from America being sighted in the Naples area within the past week.

At this point, what his connection was to Gene Roncalli or to the others involved in the Gibboni estate excavation...if any...was not clear. But they indicated that they would be following up the lead and keep them informed of any developments.

CHAPTER TWENTY-SIX

Angelo was giving the couple a tour of the excavation site so that they could see the progress that had been made during their absence and an estimate of what still remained to be done.

"So far, we have removed about fifty portraits and several old trunks that contain clothing that would appear to be ones worn in a number of the pictures. It is proving most interesting. I'm sure there are going to be any number of museums that would pay handsomely for this collection."

One of Angelo's men interrupted the conversation.

"Excuse me, Angelo." He doffed his hat at the pair.

"There's something here that I think all of you should see" he said.

The trio followed the worker into the depths of the basement.

"We found this small vault here in the wall. One of my crew is an expert at opening locks.

With your permission, sir?"

Angelo's enthusiasm was palpable. He looked at the couple who in turn nodded their agreement.

"Please."

The workman approached the vault, evaluated it and then with great precision had the lock disengaged in a matter of moments.

As he opened the door, they all held their breath.

Inside, lay a single large envelope.

Angelo reached into his pocket for a pair of gloves that he kept specifically for handling documents. Once he had placed them on his hands, he carefully reached into the vault and grasped the document.

On it was written in fine script:

Il ritrovatore

"What does that say?"

Maria whispered to him: "To the finder."

Angelo searched for a place to deposit the packet for examination and finding an old desk nearby, he placed a clean cloth on the desk and then laid the envelope on it with exacting care.

"One must be very careful with old documents. The paper can become very fragile with age. Drying can cause cracking and flaking into pieces even with the most delicate care."

Inside the envelope were several pages of parchment-like paper. Angelo carefully extracted them.

"It's a good thing they were not folded. It can be virtually impossible to unfold old documents without them falling into pieces. And words that happen to fall in the creases often are impossible to decipher."

He very carefully lifted the top cover page and placed it aside. The pages that followed had been written by someone with impeccable penmanship in modern Italian. The date of the missive was eighteen ninety-three.

Angelo turned to the others.

"I will need some time to process the pages and translate them into English for you. There are at least five lengthy pages in rather small hand print. I can tell you though that the author was Michele Catalano...just like the one known as **Il Padrino** on the first portrait that we encountered here!"

He pointed to the signature on the final page.

*

"Luigi, at the risk of you being recognized, I'm going to send you to the Gibboni estate to see how far along they are with the basement excavation. Since our 'guest' told us what they are doing,

I think it best to let them finish and then decide how to handle things from there. There are too many people at the site right now to try anything. When the workers are through and gone, we will only have to deal with the important ones…the ones that I need to convince to keep the family story to themselves."

"You're the boss."

"Now, here's what I want you to do."

*

Angelo had been working intently on the letter for more than a day. He now had copies of the translation prepared for each of the principals.

The couple, along with the mayor, Gina and Gene Roncalli, all sat with their copies as Angelo read from his notes.

"Essentially, the Catalano family has been in charge of things around here for about three centuries. The names Michele, Antonio and Francesco are repeated almost every generation so it may be a little difficult to get things in correct order when we try to match up the portraits, unless they are dated. We'll probably need someone with expertise in clothing from the different periods to try to pinpoint times.

It seems that the **Il Padrino** title came about when Don Francesco Catalano acquired a protection scheme during hard financial times in the early seventeenth century, having killed the reigning Don, Bartolo Cenci. He was originally called Il Coltello, having killed Cenci with a knife. This was later changed to Il Padrino, or Godfather, a much more suitable name. From that time on, until this letter was written in eighteen ninety-three, every generation of Catalanos has had a designated son, usually the first born, who inherited the title, **Il Padrino**. But Michele… the one who wrote this letter…tired of the constant threats to himself and his family and not wanting to pass the title to his son, Felice, emigrated to America to avoid being taken into custody. The coming of Risorgimento…the unification of Italy…sounded the death knell to most of the organized crime families of the day… if only temporarily.

Michele's wife ***was*** Agostina Gibboni, and this was her father's estate. It seems that the family hid here in the basement for several years until they finally had to leave the country as threats to their welfare became impossible to ignore.

Michele sent part of the family to New York the year before this letter was written. He and his son Felice remained behind because they felt they might be recognized by authorities if they tried to escape through Naples and thus put the whole family in jeopardy. So at the time of the writing of this letter, Michele and Felice were departing for southern Italy or possibly Sicily to seek an alternate route to America.

And that's where it ends."

Angelo surveyed the others.

"I guess that's why I've never been able to find my grandfather on the Ellis Island census material. Apparently he didn't enter the country that way."

He looked at Maria.

"But we've now made the connection that you sought. You now have written evidence that connects Don Francesco Catalano to your known direct ancestors, Michele and Felice and to the Gibbonis through the marriage of Michele and Agostina.

There will be pieces to fill in, but all in all I'd say that your trip to Italy has begun to pay off big time."

She grabbed him by the neck and gave him a big hug and kiss.

He smiled, hugged her back and suddenly realized what a fortuitous meeting this had been for the both of them in so many ways.

CHAPTER TWENTY-SEVEN

"Well, that's the last of the portraits" Angelo affirmed with an air of satisfaction as the final picture was removed from the basement to the patio tent en route to the garage where the preliminary work of cleaning and classifying the objects was progressing.

"You've done a marvelous job" they both commented.

"I don't know how we'll ever repay you for all your time and expertise."

"Let me worry about that" Angelo retorted. "I'm not cheap you know" he said with a smile.

"Besides, I've already mentioned that these pictures will be valuable to any number of museums...and there's nothing like having your name associated with a major collection find...all of our names that is" he exclaimed while rotating his arm in a circle indicating himself and the couple.

Maria looked at her fiancé.

"My name shouldn't be included. It's your family and Angelo's work on the project that should be so honored."

He took her hand in his.

"But my dear Maria, you *will* be part of the family long before these objects adorn any museum wall."

He leaned over and kissed her lightly on the cheek.

"Well, perhaps you have a point there."

"Angelo, how long do you anticipate that the rest of your work might take?"

He got a flustered look on his face.

"Whew! That's a tough one to answer. It could be weeks or even months or more. It partially depends on how quickly the other experts we will need to help us in the identification process can get here and how long it takes them to do their work.

You see my dilemma in trying to give you an exact answer.

Now, we need to make one final inspection of the basement and make sure there is nothing that was missed. Then, we'll restore things to their original state. That will probably occupy the rest of the week. Once done, we can return the equipment that Gene Roncalli secured for us and turn the estate back into Gina Cerasale's hands.

As they were talking, a vehicle appeared in the driveway.

A solitary figure emerged and walked their way.

"My name is Luigi...Donzoni. I am looking for the Gibboni estate.

Have I come to the right place?"

Angelo approached him and extended his hand.

"My name is Angelo, and this is the Gibboni estate.

What exactly can I can help you with?"

"I was told that you might have some work here for someone with skills in excavating artifacts."

"I'm afraid that you are too late...Luigi. We have finished with that portion of the job.

How did you come to know of our work here?"

Luigi hesitated a moment.

"An acquaintance of someone from the estate...I don't know the name... mentioned it to a friend of mine."

Sensing that it would be better to curtail his conversation with the trio, he thanked Angelo for his time and turned to leave.

"Grazie" he said.

"Perhaps another time."

Then he returned to his car and immediately left.

*

Angelo turned to the pair with an annoyed look on his face.

"I don't know who else knows about our find or how they would have heard about it.

I certainly don't like outsiders coming in like this.

It makes me a little nervous."

Maria had a worried look on her face.

"It bothers me too...especially since I think I recognize that man.

I'm reasonably sure that he is one of the men that was following us in Florence some weeks ago."

She turned toward her fiancé.

"I believe you're right. His face looks familiar even to me."

*

Luigi returned immediately to the retreat in the mountains between Eboli and Campagna.

"They're almost done, Boss. They're finishing up the portrait removal and will be restoring the basement and staircase in the next few days.

Then they'll dismiss the workers."

"And that will be our cue to move in" he replied.

"I'll have a three finger scotch. And get me one of those Cuban cigars I like.

In fact, help yourselves to something too, boys. And then join me on the patio.

Our time is almost here."

*

The Eboli Polizia had interviewed Gene Roncalli and now Maria and her fiancé once again. Their stories had the common denominator centered on the gathering of information about the Catalanos and Gibbonis. The connection...if any... to someone known to be affiliated with organized crime in America was raised and remained one of the questions that went unanswered.

The police had not been successful in locating the specific mob figure thought to have been seen arriving in Naples, although their sources indicated that he may be close by. For obvious reasons, they chose not to reveal his possible identity.

The "Luigi" person who had appeared at the Gibboni estate ostensibly looking for work...the one recognized both by Maria and her fiance...could not be identified either. The name that he had given them was obviously bogus.

Following the interview, Maria suggested that she and Jack take a breather while Angelo and the police continued their respective jobs.

"Why don't you let me show you around Naples? We hardly saw anything the first time there. We've been so busy chasing all around the country in search of the Catalanos that you missed most of the city that I like to think of as home.

It really is lovely."

"I don't know. It may not be safe just now, considering what happened to Gene Roncalli.

And now we have the added worry of this Luigi character showing up at the estate."

"Why don't we contact the police and see what they recommend?"

He acquiesced.

"I'll call them. But, if they think it's a bad idea, then we stay here."

She agreed.

*

The Polizia felt that as long as the couple kept them informed of their whereabouts at all times that they should be safe. The inspector in charge made sure that he had Maria's cell phone number and that she had his so that they could be in instant contact if there were any pressing news from either side.

With that assurance, the couple returned briefly to her home in Campagna to gather their things and then proceeded to Naples.

"I suppose you've chosen another grand hotel for our stay here?" he commented as the outskirts of the city of Naples came into view.

Maria turned and looked at him in a curious way.

"How did you happen to choose the term 'grand'?"

"You know...luxurious...that kind of grand...much like the hotels you took me to along the Amalfi coast."

"Oh!

Well, it just so happens that my favorite hotel here in Naples is called the Grand Hotel Vesuvio.

That's why I asked."

As they proceeded through the old city, he commented on some of the very unkempt portions.

"It's much like other old large cities. It has many areas that the upper crust locals are not very proud of. Tourists are generally steered away from them. But, it's all part of the city I know and love."

She continued through the often narrow and curved streets until they approached the Bay of Naples. She turned onto the Via Partenope that led them to the hotel's magnificent entrance.

She drove under the porte cochere where they were met by a concierge.

"Welcome back, Ms. Fortunato" he said with a slight bow.

"Will you be staying long this time?"

She hesitated for a moment at the sound of the foreign name.

"It's Mrs. Rosato, Alberto.

"And just for a few days, thank you."

"My apologies, Mrs. Rosato.

My mistake" replied Alberto.

She introduced him to her fiancé.

He then escorted the couple into the foyer where Maria was again welcomed by name by the hotel manager himself.

"Thank you for calling ahead. We have your usual suite ready for you."

Maria introduced her fiance to the gentleman who then personally escorted them to the Caruso Suite. He recounted the history of the suite and the origin of the name as they made their way.

"If you should need anything else, please call Alberto."

They thanked him as they stepped into the oversized suite with a commanding view of the Bay of Naples.

"What was that 'Ms. Fortunato' business all about?

And did Enrico Caruso really stay here?"

"I'm not sure. He must have confused me with someone else momentarily."

She quickly jumped to answer his second question in great detail.

"Caruso lived the last several years of his life in this very suite. Of course, the hotel was destroyed during the Allied bombing toward the end of World War II and restored during the post war years. It reopened in 1950 and has hosted famous people from all over the world since then including Grace Kelly and her husband, Prince Ranier; movie stars like Humphrey Bogart and Lauren Bacall; and politicians like your President Clinton and his wife...and many others."

"Do you think they all made love in this very bed?"

"I don't know, but I'm reasonably sure we can add our names to the list of those who have, if you like?" she quickly added.

"It's been far too long" she said as she fell into his arms.

"Yes. Too long. Forget the family business for now.

Tonight, it's just you and me."

CHAPTER TWENTY-EIGHT

She had seen the sights of Napoli countless times, but Maria still enjoyed playing tour guide for those fortunate souls who came to see her city for the first time, or were returning for a more intimate look at its many famous sites.

On their initial excursion months earlier, the couple had visited several select locations that were predicated on his search for information about the Catalano family, commencing with Gaetano Catalano and Don Pedro of Toledo...a quest that had quickly led them out of the city to various parts of Italy and had culminated in the findings at the Gibboni estate.

All that remained was to await Angelo's assessment of the portraits that had been extracted from the basement. Hopefully this information would allow the family history to be placed in chronological order up to and including the present.

And while they awaited those results, they would enjoy the scenery of Naples and the surrounding area.

*

"What is that thing over there?

It looks like an old castle."

From their balcony where they sat enjoying breakfast on their first morning in Naples, he pointed to the structure adjacent to the Grand Hotel Vesuvio.

"That my love is the Castel dell'Ovo! It sits on its own little island called Megerides and is attached to the city by a causeway. It dates to the sixth century B.C. and is thought to be the original site of the city of Naples. People from Cumae historically were responsible for the original construction, but over the years numerous structures have been built on the site, including one by the Normans and most recently by the Spanish Aragonese in the fifteenth century...the one you're seeing now.

I was planning on taking you there today."

He glanced her way brandishing a great big smile.

"It's so wonderful having my own tour guide...and such a lovely one at that.

The name...what does it mean?

It sounds like it ought to have something to do with eggs."

"You're exactly right.

There is a legend that the poet Virgil, reputed to have been a sorcerer, placed magic eggs in its foundation.

But the best part of visiting it is the view you get of Naples and the bay.

So perhaps we should get going?

I've planned quite a few stops both in and out of town that I think you will find most interesting."

"Lead on.

I'm all yours."

*

The view of Naples from the Castel dell'Ovo was at least as spectacular as Maria had promised. They spent about an hour there followed by a drive past the Castel Nuovo, built by Charles of Anjou around the year twelve eighty, then finished the morning at the Capodimonte Museum.

The structure was begun in seventeen thirty-eight by Charles III of Spain as a summerhouse for royalty. It was later converted into the premier museum of the city, housing paintings by Renaissance masters such as Raphael, Titian, Caraveggio and El Greco.

The porcelain bearing the same name Capodimonte was originally made in a factory adjacent to the museum.

Midday church bells were peeling by the time they arrived at a small café fronting the thoroughfare known as Spaccanapoli, the narrow street that divides Naples from East to West. At the

Piazza del Gesu Nuovo, it joins the old Greek portion of Naples (Neapolis) with the ancient Spanish remnants.

"Well, what do you think of my city?"

"It's a lot older than I imagined. But I guess I should have known that.

The parts of town you've shown me today pre-date even those old churches we saw on our first visit.

I must admit that it's quite charming...and so very romantic in your company."

"You're too kind, my love" she said reaching for his hand.

"Now! I'm hungry and I know you must be.

How about a pizza Margherita?

It originated here in Naples, named for Queen Margherita, the wife of King Umberto I and mother of King Emmanuel III.

It's made with red tomatoes, green basil and white cheese and symbolizes the tri-color flag of Italy."

He laughed.

"I think you could sell sand to a Bedouin.

How could I possibly refuse?"

*

The pizza was even more delicious than he expected. Since he and Maria had met, everything in Italy seemed agreeable to him. She insisted that he try their *tiramisu*, the dessert that he had come to appreciate even more during his time with her.

Tiramisu freely translated means "a little pick-me-up" and Maria had certainly come to mean just that for him.

"We need to keep a list of all the places where we've tried this and decide on our favorite. Then sometime in the future we can go back on an anniversary to celebrate."

"You say the sweetest things. You certainly know how to keep a girl romantically inclined."

As they sat enjoying a cup of espresso, she suddenly looked at her watch and grabbed his hand.

"We'd better get going if we're going to make it to Cumae today."

"Cumae?

Didn't you mention that name earlier today in regard to something?"

"Well it shows that you've been paying attention."

She smiled.

"Yes.

The people that founded the city of Naples at the site of Castel dell'Ovo were from there.

It's not too far, but it's best that we take the train. Parking can be a problem some days if there are a lot of tourists.

We can walk to termini…the central train station…it's only a few blocks from here. By rail, we can be in Cumae within the hour."

"Once again, I'm all yours.

You lead and I'll follow."

*

Cumae was unlike anything he had seen either in Italy or any other country that he had visited. It had been founded in the eighth century B.C. and was the origin of the Cumean alphabet, the precursor of Latin. Its main attraction was the Cave at Cumae, discovered in 1932, and purported to be the home of the Cumean Sybil. There were several Sybils in ancient times…priestesses in charge of oracles.

The Sybil of Cumae was most famous, having been mentioned in the *Aeneid*.

As they entered the Cave, the guide pointed out that the passage they traversed was over one hundred and thirty meters long and led to the inner chamber which the Sybil occupied and from where she issued her prophesies.

"Cumae is probably the oldest known settlement in all of Italy" she said as they exited the cave.

"Have you had enough for one day?

What do you say we catch the train back to the city and then relax in the room for a while before supper?"

Her meaning was crystal clear to him and he quickly nodded in agreement.

*

The evening was sexually gratifying and an appropriate prelude to a romantic and sumptuous dinner in the Caruso Room.

"Now, tomorrow I want to take you to Capua to see the ruins of the amphitheater and the old gladiatorial school where Spartacus trained and began his revolt against Rome.

You are familiar with his story I presume?"

"Yes. Of course.

The movie is one of my favorites. I think Kirk Douglas and Jean Simmons were perfectly cast in the lead parts.

I always felt their kind of love was what I would want...and now have found.

I just hate the way it had to end for them."

Maria nodded her agreement. She hated gruesome scenes in movies and chose to not discuss it further.

Fortunately, he changed the subject abruptly.

"Perhaps we should check with Angelo and see how things are progressing at the estate?"

"I'll call him first thing in the morning. If he's ready for our return, we can go directly there from Capua.

"But right now mister, I think your comment about the love you've found needs a little reward."

*

A big reward...and a little sleep was indeed all he got. The romantic flavor of Naples was all pervasive and certainly didn't shy away from the couple's bed chamber.

Early the next morning they were up and enjoying breakfast on the terrace.

She placed a call to Angelo and was informed by him of the excellent progress he had made in the identification process, and while far from complete he wanted to share with them what he had found.

She promised him they would return by late that day, spend the night at her home in Campagna and meet for breakfast early the following morning at the Gibboni estate.

"Well I guess this means that we'd better pack our things and bid farewell to Naples" he added with a sigh.

They were on their way to Capua before eleven a.m.

*

"So, this is the famous gladiator school that boasts Spartacus as a graduate?" he commented while surveying the remains of the once famous institute.

"It doesn't look like I anticipated. It's not quite like it was portrayed in the movie."

"Things rarely look the same unless they are filmed on site, or actual film can be used…you know, like actual bombing sequences that were used in several of the Pearl Harbor movies."

They walked around the designated areas and then drove by the remnants of the large amphitheater located nearby.

"Well" Maria commented, "if you think you've seen enough, then I guess this will end our tour.

Next time we'll have to do Pompeii and Herculaneum…the cities that got in the way of Mt. Vesuvius when it erupted in seventy-nine A.D."

He smiled in her direction.

"I know.

There I go acting like a tour guide again."

"I wouldn't have it any other way.

Let's go home."

CHAPTER TWENTY-NINE

The miles back to Campagna were pleasantly uneventful and the evening spent at home passed in relative quietude. The trip to Naples had been exhilarating but it had been equally exhausting. They both slept well and awoke refreshed the next morning ready for the adventures of the day.

They arrived at the Gibboni estate by ten a.m. to find the last of the equipment being loaded onto trucks for return to the rental companies.

Angelo gave the couple a hearty greeting.

"Come, my friends, let us share breakfast and then I will show you the restoration progress.

Afterward I will let you see what we have accomplished with the portraits. I think you will be pleased."

Gina's staff had prepared an incomparable breakfast that was served on the terrace since it was a warm and sunny morning.

When they had finally finished their espresso, he led them to the closet that had yielded the stairway to the treasure laden basement where now everything appeared to have been returned to its original state.

"You've done an amazing job" they both confided to him.

"I somehow never really thought it could all be restored to its original state when I saw how they had torn everything apart in order to enlarge the opening."

"Secretly, Maria, I was a little skeptical myself.

But, I must give credit to Gene Roncalli for coming to my rescue with his knowledge of the architecture and his local business connections that got us the equipment we needed so quickly and the expertise to have done such a remarkable job."

Maria interrupted him abruptly.

"How is Gene?

Is he still here?"

"No need to worry.

He's fine.

His headache must have been related to some drugs his captors used on him. It was gone by the next morning.

He left the following day since he had business in Naples. As you know, he missed his flight to Cairo, so he had to make contact with his clients there and reschedule his trip.

I think he must be there now."

"Will he be returning here anytime soon?" she asked.

"I'm sure if the Eboli police find anything, he will need to return there. But he didn't say anything specifically about returning to Campagna or here to the estate...unless we need his help."

Maria looked disappointed.

Jack couldn't help but notice her look of displeasure and briefly felt pangs of jealously.

Then he smiled inwardly as he reminded himself that he was the fortunate one who was going to marry her...and need not be unduly concerned about a person they most likely would never see again.

*

Angelo led the couple down the restored staircase to the now empty basement. He illuminated the darkened area and led them through the vacant space.

As they approached the end of the main corridor and entered the now deserted living area, the trio could hear faint noises emanating from the floor above. Assuming it was only the house staff tending to cleaning duties that were performed daily, they continued with their tour.

As they were returning towards the stairwell, preparing to return to the main level, the lights were suddenly extinguished, throwing the entire basement into total darkness.

Their initial assumption was that there had been a power failure, although the immediate cause wasn't clear since the weather had been perfect. It might have simply been a momentary overload that had tripped a circuit breaker.

They also considered the possibility that an accident might have destroyed a power line somewhere between the estate and the source of their electricity to the south.

They joined hands in the dungeon-like atmosphere and continued cautiously towards the staircase, when a blinding light suddenly shone brightly into their eyes.

They realized they were not alone!

*

"Well" the baritone voice said.

"We finally meet."

Jack instinctively grabbed for Maria's shoulder and pulled her to him.

He felt a sudden shudder run through his body and Maria's as well.

Angelo remained silent.

Suddenly, the room was inundated with light, revealing the source of the voice. Next to him stood two other men.

They promptly recognized one…the man calling himself Luigi who had come to the estate purportedly looking for work just days earlier…the same one that they both agreed had been shadowing them in Florence.

The apparent leader, the one who spoke with the baritone voice, walked toward them while Luigi and the other man fanned out around the trio.

Luigi held his right hand in his pocket apparently palming a gun.

"So!

Just what made you decide to come here and stick your noses into my family's long guarded secret?"

"Do I know you?" he queried.

"No!

But I know you and your kind…meddling into other people's business when you have no right to."

"But that's not true…I have every reason to be here.

I came to find out about my ancestors.

Doesn't everyone want to explore their family history and find out where they came from?"

The one in charge remained silent and motionless.

"You still haven't answered my question.

I still don't know your name?"

"My name is Salvatore Catalano, but perhaps you would know me better as 'Toto'. It was you who called my home in New York and talked to my sister many months ago."

"So you are the famous 'Toto' Catalano.

Well, that's was just an honest mistake. I was given your home number by a relative…obviously it was a big 'honest' mistake.

I think we are distantly related though…in fact, I'm sure we must be given your interest in the Gibbonis and Catalanos.

Toto, my name is John Catalano McDaniel.

But, I'm better known as Jack to my friends.

My mother was Elena Catalano. Her father was Felix Catalano and he was born here in Campagna. She married my father, James McDaniel, from Georgia.

Michele Catalano was my great-grandfather and Agostina Gibboni was my great-grandmother."

Toto appeared stunned by the revelation.

"Agostina was my great-grandmother too" he said, with a touch of nostalgia in his voice.

As they continued their exchange of family information, a clamor suddenly erupted from the stairwell.

Four men brandishing automatic weapons descended into the room and immediately took charge.

"Drop your weapons" one of the group demanded of Toto and his men.

Realizing that they were overpowered, Toto and his small band cowered against the wall of the hallway and immediately dropped their guns to the floor.

"What took you so long to get here?"

Angelo, Jack, Toto and his men all looked askance at the source of the voice.

"Sorry, Ms. Fortunato.

We've been tracking your friend here and finally realized who he was.

We wanted to make absolutely sure that we would have things under control when we arrived."

He waved the automatic weapon in his hand as he spoke.

Jack turned toward Maria in stunned silence!

CHAPTER THIRTY

Jack continued to stare silently at Maria as she walked toward the man holding the weapon.

"I don't think those will be necessary, Roberto."

She moved her hands in a downward direction indicating that it was safe to put the guns away.

Roberto signaled the others to do the same.

Toto turned and approached her once the guns had been secured and he no longer felt threatened.

"So you are the famous Maria Fortunato!

I had always heard that you were a beautiful woman but no one had made the comparison to Sophia Loren.

Obviously, I would have recognized you if they had."

"It's nice to finally meet one of my American capos" she replied.

"I was pleased to hear that you had been released from prison and were able to return to the organization."

The others stood in silence, not fully comprehending the conversation that they were hearing.

Maria walked toward Jack and took his hand.

"I know that what I am about to tell you and the others won't make sense at first, but perhaps you will understand if you listen to the whole story before coming to any illogical conclusions."

She tightened her hold on Jack's hand and whispered into his ear.

"Understand that even if my story sounds unbelievable, know that my love for you is real and that we can work things out."

Jack wasn't sure how to respond.

He momentarily withdrew his hand from hers and stood back as he prepared to listen to her story.

*

"You see, when I married my late husband, Paulo Rosato, I was young and naïve. He told me that he was a dealer in antiquities and historical artifacts…and that was at least partially true. It was the front for his real profession as head of the Mafia in Campania. I didn't know much about that until the year before his death… before he was killed."

Turning towards Jack, she continued.

"I told you that he had died after suffering a heart attack while driving and that his car struck a bridge abutment.

Well …that was also partly the truth.

What really happened was that an opposition gang from Tuscany set him up for a hit since Paulo's people had dared cross the line into the southern part of their region. They rigged an explosive on one of the wheels of his car. When it went off, he lost control of the vehicle and hit the bridge abutment, killing him instantly.

By that time, I was fully aware of his activities and had been introduced to all of his constituents in Naples and the surrounding area. Following his death, they elected me to fill the position of acting head in the region. It seemed logical since I was free to move about at will, especially with my resemblance to a famous movie star.

And they felt that a woman would not be suspected of leading the Mafia.

In addition to Naples and Campania, we have abundant ties to America, especially in New York City."

Once again she turned to her fiancé, Jack.

"You know, the 'pizza connection.'"

Suddenly, things were beginning to make sense.

"Toto here is our main link in the New York and New Jersey area…but we've never met until now. I recognized him from pictures I had seen but felt it best to let him introduce himself.

When I recognized Luigi in Florence, I contacted Roberto. He's been keeping an eye on him. We knew that Toto had arrived in Naples recently, but didn't want to make a move until we were sure he was coming here.

I knew it must have been Toto and his men that kidnapped Gene Roncalli, but I didn't want to reveal my identity to the police. So I just let them proceed alone. Fortunately, they were slow as usual in solving the mystery...in fact, they still haven't!"

"Ms. Fortunato...."

"Please, Toto, call me Maria.

Everyone else does."

Seeing the lingering confused look on Jack's face, she paused to clarify the facts about her name.

"Jack, my maiden name was Maria Fortunato. After Paulo was murdered, we felt it best not to use the Rosato name any longer."

"So that's why at the hotel in...."

"Yes. I thought they were going to give me away. I had been back several times since Paulo's death and had used my 'new name.'"

She turned back to Toto.

"Go ahead.

Now you tell your story."

"I'm sorry that I didn't recognize you, Maria.

But I have a story to tell too concerning my ancestors here in this place and why my men were tracking you and your fiancé.

You see, my ancestors...our ancestors" he added looking at Jack, "distinguished themselves in the Campania region over the past three centuries by running protection rackets under the guise of legitimate banking, and simultaneously leading bands of criminals on marauding raids all over southern Italy.

It all began with Francesco Catalano, the first **Il Padrino** or 'godfather' and then passed to each inheriting son beginning with his son, Michele.

It was our mutual great-grandmother's husband, another Michele Catalano that decided to put a stop to it by leaving Italy and immigrating to America in the eighteen-nineties.

Now unfortunately, after I left Italy and went to New York, I became involved with some less than desirable people...the Mafia to be exact. I eventually was apprehended and put in prison for over ten years. During my incarceration, I decided that I had had enough of living as a criminal and resolved to change my ways.

I'm truly ashamed of what I've done, and I purposefully leave no male heirs to carry on my name. I was hoping that these secrets buried here in Campagna could remain hidden from the rest of the family and the world.

Unfortunately, the last Gibboni died and insisted on that portrait being placed in the museum...and Maria, you and Jack have somehow cleverly managed to discover the truth here in this house.

And you, Angelo, I'm sure must have plans to disseminate the story now that you have uncovered all the treasures that were stored here within these walls."

The entire group stood silent for a few moments.

Jack was first to break the silence.

"Toto, I commend you for your change of heart and for your willingness to share the truth with us.

But, I'm afraid that I haven't exactly been forthcoming either."

He looked directly at Maria.

"You see, I told you that I'm in the import/export business... well, like your story about your late husband Paulo, it's only partly the truth.

The fact of the matter is...I import drugs and export small arms to rogue nations. I'm in charge of the Atlanta and southeast drug and arms cartel, but my ties are directly to the west coast since we import mostly from Central and South America and the Orient and ship most of our arms to the Middle East.

I guess the only person missing here today is a priest to hear all of our confessions."

After a brief moment to reflect on his "confession" remark, they all burst into laughter.

Jack looked at Maria and then in turn at Toto.

"I guess we have a lot to talk about" Toto remarked.

Angelo, standing amidst the trio of mob figures, surrounded by men holding various loaded weapons that rendered him helpless and vulnerable, stood silent.

Jack and Maria could see the troubled look on his face.

"My friend, please do not feel threatened by us. We are all most appreciative of what you have done for our family" said Maria.

"Let us have the opportunity to sit and talk together and decide how we will proceed from here. Then let us make you a proposal in regard to how we should handle the portraits and the family story."

Angelo nodded his agreement.

"Suppose we dismiss the men and retire to the dining room and discuss this over a glass of wine?" Maria proposed to the men.

"Agreed" they both answered.

CHAPTER THIRTY-ONE

Toto and Maria each dismissed their men. The three then sat down to formulate plans for proceeding from this point.

"This is certainly not the place that I thought we would find ourselves today," Toto stated with mirth in his manner.

Maria and Jack smiled in response.

"As I said earlier, I want the Catalano name to remain one associated with honor here in the region...as it has been for the past century or more. When I left for America, I was essentially unknown here. My criminal life began in New York...and I'm going to try to let it die there...if I can slip back out of the country without the Polizia apprehending me.

Perhaps there is some way to donate the portraits to museums without providing the full story behind each of the subjects... making them out to have been important figures in the banking industry...as they were in reality...in Campania and southern Italy."

"I think we can take the letter from Michele Catalano and keep it in a vault...perhaps to be willed to some future relation...say in a hundred years or so."

Jack turned towards Maria.

"Perhaps to one of our great-great grand children?"

She reached over and gave him a hug.

"I like that idea."

"And what's to become of the three of us and our 'careers'?"

Jack answered first directing his remarks to Maria.

"I've been thinking about that ever since my first trip here when we met. I spent most of my time back in Georgia trying to figure out how to tell you about my real career, never dreaming that we shared more in common than either of us would have dared to imagine.

I'm ready to call it quits with that business. In fact, I have already made tentative arrangements with my associates back home to take over my holdings.

There's only one major problem!

I feel that we need to divorce ourselves completely from our former lives. There's always someone who wouldn't trust us to just leave and not eventually expose them."

Maria's look indicated she didn't understand his meaning.

"Are you familiar with our F.B.I.'s witness relocation program?"

Again she looked confused.

Toto smiled, acknowledging his understanding.

"It's a program by which the F.B.I....that's our Federal Bureau of Investigation... takes people who are in jeopardy of their lives... as well we might be...and move them to new locations with new names, new careers and authentically fabricated past histories. In some cases, people even undergo plastic surgery to make themselves unrecognizable by friends and family."

Jack looked at Maria.

"You might have to consider something like that since your looks attract everyone that sees you...that is, if you would be agreeable to my suggestion.

Would you be willing to give up your position here in Italy?"

"Oh, Jack.

There's nothing that would make me happier. As I told you, this wasn't what I expected when I married Paulo. This is not the life I imagined for myself.

You know, I've been thinking about this too...and I think I have the perfect solution...Angelo."

Jack and Toto both looked perplexed at the suggestion.

"Before you ask" she continued, "I told you Angelo was on old friend of mine. Actually, he was an old friend of Paulo's. He knows all about our activities since he worked with Paulo before his death. He stayed on to work with me both in the antiquities business and the Mafia activities.

He'd be the perfect one to take over for me."

Jack looked at Toto who uttered "agree".

"You have our support if Angelo is in agreement" Jack said, placing his hand on Maria's arm.

"I think it is safe to say that this has turned into one of the strangest days of my life" added Toto.

"One additional thing" added Jack.

You know the Poliz*ia* are looking for you as we speak?"

Toto hesitated to answer, always wary of the consequences of telling the truth.

"Suppose we were to tell the police that we don't want to press charges…that we now realize that it was just a family prank?"

That made Toto smile.

"Then I think I would have to say that you are correct in your assessment of the recent events that you enquired about."

They all laughed.

"That sounds like 'gangster-speak' to me," Maria interjected.

"If we're all in agreement, let's call Angelo in and see if he's agreeable to taking over here. Then we can begin planning our new lives and you can return to New York, uneventfully, I hope" added Maria.

"Salut" said Toto as he raised his wine glass and proposed a toast to the future.

*

A final decision was made to leave the estate to Gina Cerasale. Toto declined any part of the inheritance for obvious reasons. Jack and Maria had plans to relocate as already mentioned. And she was native Italian. They didn't care to divulge the other reasons to her known only to Jack, Maria, Angelo and Toto. The only stipulation was that the majority of the reclaimed portraits be donated to the museum that was to be built with the money left to Campagna from the Gibboni estate.

That was agreeable to Gina.

CHAPTER THIRTY-TWO

Maria and Jack never regretted the decision they had made following that momentous occasion at the Gibboni estate when confessions were the order of the day.

Toto Catalano had managed to evade the police in Italy only to be apprehended in New York City as he attempted to re-enter the port. An all points bulletin had been issued by the federal authorities after receiving word of his presumed presence in Italy. Under the terms of his parole, he was not allowed to leave the country.

He was sentenced to an additional five years in confinement as a result of his actions. However, he succumbed to a heart attack six months after returning to Sing Sing prison in New York State. His promise not to further sully the reputation of the Catalano family name in Italy had been fulfilled.

Angelo eagerly agreed to take the reins of the Campania mafia, paving the way for Jack and Maria to marry and begin life anew. He was sorry to see her depart, but given the circumstances under which she had come to be affiliated with the Mafia, he couldn't help but feel that she deserved a fresh start in life.

*

"And now, it's time I made an honest woman out of you."

As soon as they had returned to her place in Campagna, Jack took Maria aside and suggested they make plans for their wedding as soon as possible.

"You pick the time and the place.

Would you prefer Italy, or Georgia? Or anywhere else in the whole wide world? It's your choice."

She thought for a few moments.

"We met here in Campagna and it is my home, so I think here would be the best place. I'm only sorry that mother isn't alive to meet you and be here for the wedding.

She would love you as I do."

He pulled her close to himself and gave her a big hug.

"And I'm sorry I didn't get to meet her if she was anything like you."

*

The wedding was a private affair performed at the small church in Campagna just days later with Angelo, Gina Cerasale and Mayor Antonio Badalementi as their witnesses. Then as promised, just as soon as Maria had settled her affairs there, Jack took her to a very special honeymoon location...in Kauai.

They flew via Rome to New York and onward to Honolulu; then the short flight to the Lihue airport on Kauai. Jack had arranged a rental car for the short drive to the Princeville area along the Kuhio Highway, allowing him to point out various sights of the island as they made their way to an estate that belonged to one of his contacts in the Middle East.

It had a commanding view of Lumahai Beach on Hanalei Bay.

"I hope you've had the opportunity to see the movie '**South Pacific**'? They stood on the prominence at the edge of the estate property gazing at the beach below.

Maria was unsure, but thought that she probably had.

"Well, this was the stretch of sand featured in the movie as 'the nurses' beach."

"It's beautiful.

I see now why you thought it would be such a special place for our honeymoon."

*

Their ten days on Kauai were filled with activity that included excursions to the island's main tourist sites, the Fern Grotto and Waimea Canyon. Maria insisted that they spend time on the beach enhancing her already natural tan.

Most of the remaining time was spent in passionate lovemaking. The pair shared a common sense of uncertainty in regard to their futures...and clung to one another tightly as they explored those feelings.

It was a time of complete sharing of their past lives prior to embarking on the new adventure that they were planning. They mutually decided on settling in a neutral country where hopefully the names Fortunato, Rosato, Catalano and McDaniel were not on anyone's wanted list.

But before departing the Hawaiian Islands, Jack decided he wanted to arrange brief stops on the mainland so that Maria might have at least one opportunity to see his native land...before they left it behind forever. They visited San Francisco and Las Vegas so that he might show her the main attractions of two of his favorite cities.

Once in Atlanta, he proudly escorted her to the city's finest sites including the upscale shopping areas of Buckhead, the grand sculpture of Confederate generals adorning the side of Stone Mountain, and the Civil War panorama at the Cyclorama. And they concluded the brief excursion with a visit to the pandas at the Atlanta Zoo.

From Atlanta, he escorted her to Savannah and to Hilton Head Island where Jack had arranged for Maria to undergo some minor facial plastic surgery that minimized her likeness to Sophia Loren.

As soon as he had completed transfer of his holdings, and all the necessary papers had been prepared for their new identities, the couple departed for Hartsfield-Jackson airport from where they would embark on their new life. As they awaited their flight boarding call, Jack turned to Maria.

"Take a last look at our former lives. From now on, Jack and Maria McDaniel no longer exist." He held up their passports displaying their new identities.

Maria held his hand tightly as tears welled up in her eyes.

*

Their flight took them from Atlanta to Kennedy airport in New York and then non-stop to Athens, Greece. After a one day layover, they went by boat to their new home on the small island of Kerkyra…or Corfu as it is known to the rest of the world, where they began their new lives.

He had arranged for them to be tutored in conversational Greek prior to departing Georgia. They both had mastered it in a matter of weeks and passed customs without difficulty.

Shortly after setting up their new home, Maria announced that she was pregnant with their first child.

PART FOUR

Fifteen years later

CHAPTER THIRTY-THREE

Alannis had just turned fourteen.

"Mom, Mrs. Iliopoulos, our English teacher assigned us a term paper project today, although it's not due for several months.

We're supposed to trace our family history back as far as we can and also write a feature about one memorable ancestor.

Can you and Dad help me with it?

You know, over all these years you really haven't spoken much about your past. I really know very little about where we come from.

I've never even met any of my grandparents or cousins or aunts and uncles, if I have any."

She spoke in her native Greek language.

Colista knew that this day would come...and she and Ianni had dreaded the very thought of it. They still weren't sure how best to handle the problem even after all the intervening years and numerous discussions about it.

"Let me discuss it with your father. I'm sure that we can pull together the information you will need.

Did your teacher give you a list of facts that she would like included in the paper?"

Alannis reached into her book bag and brought out her laptop computer. She opened up her e-mail list and clicked on the item that her teacher had sent to each of the students in her class.

"Here" she said as she set the computer on the counter and rotated the screen so that her mother could see it.

"Why don't you take it to your room and print me a copy. I'll show it to your father when he gets home and we'll discuss it with you later. He should be here soon.

In the meantime, why don't you go ahead and start on your homework?"

Alanis returned momentarily with a copy of the required items for the term paper and handed it to her mother.

"I'll call you when supper is ready, dear."

Colista glanced at the items on the list and just sighed.

*

That same evening after dinner, Colista and Ianni sat and stared at the list of items that Alannis's teacher had specified to be included in the term paper project.

"It's everything that we have struggled to protect all these years…our real family names, family origins, pertinent dates for births, deaths and marriages, and relationships (if any) to famous people.

How are we ever going to tell her the truth?"

As they reflected on their dilemma, Ianni suddenly had a thought.

"Why don't we take her to Campagna and show her where you really come from. We can show her the Gibboni estate and the museum…and tell her about me and my trip to Italy to find my roots, how we met and how it all came together there.

But, we must insist that she never divulge it to anyone except her immediate family when she has one. It would also give us a chance to see what's become of the town museum that I presume has been built by now.

For her project though, we can assist her with information that we have been using since we relocated here.

It's all authentic if anyone cares to research it.

I think that she is capable of knowing the truth and protecting our family secret, don't you?"

"Alannis has been the best daughter anyone could have asked for.

Mi Amor, I think that's a great idea.

It's no wonder that I still love you so much after all these years."

"I love it when you speak in Italian."

He pulled her close to him and cupped her breasts.

"You still like these old things after all these years? They're not so perfect as when we first met and made love there in my house in Campagna."

He held them only tighter.

"Suppose you let me be the judge of that."

"Perhaps you'd like to inspect them more closely in the bedroom?"

He laughed.

"You Italian women never change…and thank God for that!"

*

The road from Eboli to Campagna had changed little since that day more than fifteen years ago when last they had driven it… en route to their honeymoon in Hawaii and their new lives. They had presumed it would be their last glimpse of Maria's home…and Jack's ancestral homeland forever.

Yet here they were…almost home once again, and in the company of their fourteen year old daughter.

Prior to leaving Corfu, they had shared with Alannis abbreviated facts about their true identities and how they came to be Greek citizens. They briefly alluded to their involvement in some illicit activities in the past, omitting specific details hopefully for her benefit.

Maria had chosen not to mention her previous marriage to Paulo Rosato since it had ended tragically and had no bearing on Alannis's life.

Approaching the small town, there was no discernible change that they could detect except for the museum. The once small building where Maria had worked and where she and Jack had met was now a two story edifice situated on the site of the original structure. Her home was gone and the land that once held it was incorporated into a spacious parking area.

As they approached the museum entrance that faced onto the main road from Eboli, they saw the sign proclaiming the Antonio

Gibboni/Campagna Historical Museum. It pleased them that the funds purported to go for this project had indeed been used as specified in Antonio's will.

"Dad, is the museum named after the Antonio Gibboni you told me about?" Alannis innocently asked.

"Yes.

"But let's go inside and your mother and I will tell you everything you want to know.

And, as we agreed at home, this is to be privileged information for you only and no one else...until you have your own family...and then you may share it with them, only with the same provision."

Alannis agreed once again to abide by their rules.

*

As they entered, they were greeted in the foyer by a young lady wearing a tag with the name Lucia embossed on it.

"Is this your first time here to Campagna and our beautiful museum?"

"Yes", Maria answered with a half truth. It was after all their first time in the new structure and Alannis's initial visit to the town and the museum.

"Were so proud of our new facilities...we just had the dedication and grand opening celebration on the fifth of June.

If you have any questions, I would be happy to try to answer them for you.

If you would prefer to take the self guided tour, you can obtain head sets for a small fee. As you walk through the various galleries, the narrative will tell you about the portraits and other artifacts."

"Thank you, I think we would prefer to do that. If we have any questions when we're through, we'll check with you then."

Lucia smiled and showed them to the desk where they obtained their headsets.

The three looked at each other.

"It certainly took them a long time to build the facility, in the true Italian way."

Jack smiled at her comment as he took Maria's hand, and then Alannis's and led them on the tour.

"Let's see what they've done with our family history."

*

Angelo Cassavetes, aided by Eugene Roncalli, were credited as the museum chief architects in the brochure describing how the facility had come into being. The pair had done a most remarkable job of identifying and chronologically displaying the members of the Catalano family, beginning with Francesco and ending with Michele in the late eighteen hundreds.

The genealogical connections to the original Catalano...Don Gaetano...and his prominence in the history of Naples and of Italy dating to the early fifteen hundreds were prominently chronicled as well. Large portraits of him, along with those of Charles V, King of Spain and his Viceroy, Don Pedro of Toledo, adorned the wall of the final chamber before the tour took them back to a small room adjacent to the entrance foyer.

Here was displayed a portrait of the museums benefactor, Antonio Gibboni.

Jack gazed at his ancestor and turned to Alannis.

"This is your great-great grandfather.

His daughter, Agostina Gibboni, married Michele Catalano... his was the portrait you saw earlier...and together they had Felice, my grandfather.

They are the ones that left Italy in the eighteen nineties and went to America. I came to Campagna because of them, seeking my past.

And that is how I came to meet and marry your mother. And together with the help of Angelo Cassavetes and Eugene Roncalli, this is what we discovered about my family.

And now you know where you come from.

Pretty impressive, huh?

But, it must remain our secret."

Alannis was overwhelmed. She repeated her promise once again to faithfully honor the family secret.

*

They turned their attention to the solid steel safe ensconced within the wall just below the portrait. The inscription on it read:

"Contained in this safe are documents to be opened on the one hundredth anniversary of the museum...in the year 2115. The documents are purported to contain information about the Gibboni and related families that was thought too sensitive to be opened at the time of Antonio Gibboni's death."

"Dad, what do you suppose the letter says?"

"Some day your mother and I will tell you all about the contents of the letter in this safe."

Alannis looked at him with a quizzical expression.

"But how could you know...?"

"We'll share all that with you at the proper time."

*

As they were about to exit the facility, Lucia approached Jack.

"Are you sure you've never been here before?

There seems to me to be a resemblance between you and the subjects of several of our portraits.

Are you somehow related?"

"You know, I've been accused of resembling a variety of people over the years, and at one time my wife here was often mistaken for Sophia Loren."

Lucia smiled.

As she studied Maria's face, years following plastic surgery and now showing the signs of age and sun exposure, Lucia saw no similarities at all.

"No" Jack emphatically concluded.

"We've never been here before. All my ancestors are Greek.

But thank you for the compliment.

They were handsome men for their times."

The trio exited the museum and bade Campagna farewell for the very last time.

PART FIVE

June 5, 2115

Chapter Thirty-Four

Iannis grew to womanhood, keeping the secrets she had learned in Campagna that day in 2015 deep in her heart. When she was twenty-seven, she married a young Greek man by the name of Demetrios Christopoulos with whom she bore one son.

Appropriately, he was named Ianni after his grandfather.

Both Ianni and Colista had lived long lives in their self imposed isolation on the island of Corfu. Fortunately, they were never troubled by haunts from their past lives. He had become a successful financier while Colista was content to be "just" a housewife, although she did dabble in painting seascapes, scenes that were mostly visible from the terrace of their home situated on a hillside on the eastern end of the island.

Each had died within months of one other some forty years after their relocation to Greece. They had lived long enough to see their grandson grow to manhood. Now almost seventy himself, he was fulfilling the promise made to his grand-parents that he would return to Campagna for the one hundreth anniversary celebration of the Gibboni museum and the opening of the safe containing the letter that he had heard so much about from them and his mother.

Since he had never married and had no heirs, the Catalano saga would end with his death if not for the letter about to be revealed to the world.

*

It was a warm and sunny Wednesday, the fifth of June twenty-one hundred and fifteen when Ianni Christopoulos walked into the Gibboni museum, now filled with local town dignitaries and curious onlookers from the Campania area who had come to see the contents of the safe revealed. The museum had been advertising the event for the year prior to the anniversary date in hopes of making up for flagging patronage over the preceding decades. With few if any living relatives of the Gibboni and Catalano families, interest in the facility had waned.

The dignitaries were highly pleased at the turnout and hoped it would signal a turnaround in the fortunes of the facility… depending on the contents of the letter about to be revealed. A significant number of local, national and international members of the press were present, so hopes were running high.

After numerous introductory speeches by the mayors of Campagna and Eboli and the featured guest, the mayor of Naples, the main event commenced with the museum director performing the honors.

"Ladies and gentlemen, it is my distinct honor to reveal to you the contents of this safe, placed here a century ago at the request of our benefactor, Antonio Gibboni's immediate family, and members of his related family, the Catalanos.

So without further ado, I am going to proceed."

The combination to the safe had been carefully preserved. He held the document in his hand with the numbers printed on it.

The digits were properly sequenced and the handle turned.

The anticipation in the crowd was palpable.

"I am now opening the safe!" the director proudly announced as the door began to move.

He paused briefly as the door appeared to stick but then swung fully open. His face dropped as he saw that the hermetic seals had disintegrated over the intervening century.

From those able to see the interior of the safe a loud collective sigh filled the room!

The letter and its contents had disintegrated into tiny flakes of paper with no discernible writing left intact.

Members of the press knew they had a novel story to report and nothing more. And the museum director quickly realized that his job was over and he could begin planning closure of the facility.

But for Ianni, the Catalano family secret was forever intact.

He turned and walked out the front door, smiling to himself as he exited the facility.

He looked to the heavens, knowing that his grandparents were gazing down upon him and smiling too.

-End

ABOUT THE AUTHOR

John R. "Jack" Langley is a general and vascular surgeon who has been engaged in locum tenens surgery for the past fifteen years. He currently lives in Georgia with Janet, his wife of fifty years; Christian and Cashlynn, their two grandchildren; and three Tonkinese cats. This will be his fifth novel in print.